G R JORDAN

Water's Edge

A Highlands and Islands Detective Thriller

To Jean for all your support.
At last one in a genre you favour.

Contents

Foreword

This story is set in the idyllic yet sometimes harsh landscape of the Isle of Lewis, located in the north-western part of Scotland. Although set amongst known towns and lochs, note that all persons and specific places are fictional and not to be confused with actual buildings and structures that exist and which have been used as an inspirational canvas on which to tell a completely fictional story.

Chapter 1

The dreary haar hung around the harbour limits meaning anything beyond the small lighthouse was abandoned to the grey blanket. From the top floor of the station, he could usually see right out into the Minch, even catch the odd passing cargo ship as it made its way through the often rough waters that separated the island from the mainland. At five o'clock in the morning, his shift was taking its toll and he was fighting the bleary eyes that had been forced to look at the information screens so necessary for his job.

The thing about this time of the morning was that so little happened in general, it was normally qu-. No, he must not say that word. Under no circumstances was that word to be mentioned or even thought of, lest a cavalcade of woe would come in on the emergency numbers. So far the night had been routine. Just after his shift had started, one of the visiting yachts to the area had broken down and he had been involved in organising the lifeboat to help them negotiate the entry to the harbour. Otherwise it had all been qu-, routine.

Turning back to the room from the window, he saw his colleague, her face rooted to her screen and headset on. It may have been her timesheet she was looking at, because for this time of the morning she seemed intense. But then again she was often intense, especially when anything broke the qu-, routine nature of the shift. Looking behind her, he saw the paper calendar with its simple indicator that was moved along the numbers to indicate the day. Then he baulked at the number it displayed. She hadn't moved it on at midnight. Now a day behind, he knew his mind would return to it time and again until the marker was adjusted. There was something wrong in his make-up surely, affected as he was by such simple and inconsequential things.

He turned back to the window, stretching his arms and legs, pushing back the cramping feeling attacking them. Keeping himself from tightening up was always a problem. When you sat for so long…

An artificial claxon broke the quiet of the room. On spinning round he saw the confirmatory red panel flashing and he automatically raced back to the desk. Grabbing his headset, he placed it over his ears and then pressed the red button, accepting the incoming distress call.

"Coastguard Rescue!"

"Coastguard," screamed a voice, "Is that the Coastguard?"

"Yes sir," he answered calmly whilst inside his blood began to pump fast and he felt the nervous twinge in his stomach. This sounded like a bad one. "What's the problem?"

"There's someone out there. Someone on the rocks."

"Where are you, sir?" The need to locate and then send help burned in his mind.

"I think they're dead, God, I think she's dead."

"We will get help to you, sir, but I need to know where you are. Where are you, sir?"

"Oh God, she's dead. She must be dead. I can see her throat, inside her throat. Even from here."

"Where are you? Tell me where you are, sir?"

But the phone call had dropped from the system. His heart pounded but he forced his brain to think through what to do. Position, I need a position he thought, somewhere to send teams. Looking up at the screen he saw the incident had been flagged on his map. Because it was a mobile call, it was showing an indicative position, not necessarily accurate but based on a mobile mast and the information garnered electronically during the call. Start there, he thought, just start there.

Standing, he started issuing instructions to his colleague and shouted for their third watch keeper to come back in from their break. He requested they send a lifeboat, coastal rescue teams and a helicopter, treating the casualty as still alive despite the caller's assertion. Then he called the mobile phone that the first informant, the man who had been so panicked, had called in on. But it just rang out.

As the wheels of search and rescue spun rapidly, he realised that this was no longer a qu..., routine night shift.

Chapter 2

Detective Inspector Macleod sat in one corner of the station's cafeteria with his eyes closed. He could hear the clatter of knives and forks, spooning down of greasy breakfasts and cereals, coffee cups lifting and descending but he was in his own calm and serene island. It was always good to start a day with prayer and he had done so when he had arisen. But now as he waited for his colleague to join him, he indulged in some more brief moments with his Lord.

There was so much in this world that needed fixing, his day job told him that. Twenty years on the force and now working the murder squad, he had seen plenty, unlike the upstart that was about to join him. In recent years, everything had gone crazy. He had worked with women before, most of them more than competent at their jobs, indeed some had even been the reason they had solved certain cases. But he had grown up with women knowing their role in the home and this was a change he had found hard to swallow.

Yet, he had swallowed it, to the point that his senior officer was a woman and he showed no resentment or annoyance but instead had worked with her the best he could. It helped that she was very professional, knew him and his job. And so, despite the many reservations he had, he worked with this new openness the force displayed.

However, the woman about to join him was different. In her mid-twenties, she had risen up the ranks quickly and was now a detective, recently assigned to his department. Although he had never worked directly with her, he had seen her about, usually in something provocative and unashamed to flirt. And not just with the men. There were rumours that she was quite hedonistic in her life but he had never seen the point of investigating this further as his boss had seen the sense of never assigning her to a team of his. But with Mackenzie having been taken off-line after the car crash, there was no choice but to pair them.

His eyes opened and he baulked at the flesh in front of his face. There were two buttons undone on her blouse and he was sure he could see a bra strap. As his head lifted he looked into the youthful face that smiled back at him. Her red hair was tied back in a ponytail and around her neck hung a simple gold chain on which hung a small cross. Inside something raged that this precious symbol was being hijacked by this woman but he knew he had to maintain his calm.

"Detective McGrath, thank you for your punctuality. I think it's time we get to the airport, I believe the flight to Lewis leaves in a little less than two hours."

The woman nodded. "Of course, but please call me Hope. I think using long titles just gets in the way, sir."

Nodding, he rose from his own chair. *Sir, that's good*, he thought, *formal enough, she's not getting to call me Seoras*. Placing the chair back under the table, he saw one of the uniformed officers approach and hand Hope a small package. When the officer had gone, he asked her what it was.

"Just some photos from the convention I attended. Comic books, sir." She took some out of the packet and handed them to Macleod. Looking at the first one, he saw her in a group of girls all dressed in bright, bold outfits. This was not an issue but the amount of body left uncovered was. Still, he couldn't lecture her straight away about where this path would take her.

"Very good," he said mutedly, "but we can't stand around. There's a body that wants to talk to us." Hope nodded and he knew she got his point.

Routing via the office, they grabbed their small cases and were then taken by Johnstone to the airport. There would be a small team by the time everyone arrived but himself and Hope would be there as quickly as possible. The local officers would be holding the fort until then and he hoped they wouldn't do anything daft. Deep inside, he knew this attitude towards the resident force was just a front for his nervousness about returning home, back to the island that had been his childhood home, a place he had not seen in over twenty years.

Waiting in the lounge, secreted down a small staircase, he looked around at the island faces about to board the small aeroplane with him. Someone had said the cross winds at Stornoway would make the landing fun and he remembered their devilish face, almost gloating in his apprehension at flying. The winged coach held just over thirty seats and he would be seated beside Hope in the cabin. Trying to focus his thoughts on the case before him, he found himself thinking of falling through the air, or seeing the plane run off the runway and then exploding into flames. Irrational and childish he knew, but he couldn't beat these demons from his door.

"Coffee, sir."

Hope was holding a paper cup before him and he gratefully took it. Watching her then walk over to the long window to stare at the airport workings, he saw several other men stare at her behind. When she turned round suddenly, he noticed their eyes quickly divert before commencing to stare again. There was no doubt that she was extremely attractive but Macleod felt that she flaunted her looks. When he was growing up, girls kept their legs covered and certainly showed no hint of breastbone never mind any lingerie peering out. She may not have been the most buxom woman he had ever seen but there was no need to offer them up like a sacrifice on the altar of men's thoughts.

The Tannoy system broke into life and Macleod chuckled internally at the fact that the speaker was only ten feet away from his audience and yet was using this device to be heard. Standing with his ticket, he was flanked by Hope and he wondered how it must look to others, a slip of a girl as his companion. No, she was no "slip" of a girl. Detective McGrath was almost six foot, and although reasonably broad, did not have an obvious ounce of fat on her. Maybe it was because she was in the prime of life, a time when even he had so little wrong with his physical appearance. No, everyone was probably thinking they were work colleagues. The thought that people were surmising he was a dirty old man, was not one to be entertained.

The aircraft rolled down the runway and glided into the sky, but was then buffeted by some rough winds. Macleod swallowed hard trying to keep a solemn appearance. His ears were being assaulted by the noise of the engines and he suddenly realised McGrath was talking to him. She seemed to be asking if he was alright but was leaning forward and he found the scent of her perfume invading his nostrils. It was subtle and pleasant, intoxicating to a degree and coupled with her neckline, it gave him a warm sensation. But it was wrong and he looked away from her, holding a hand up to indicate no help was required.

Thankfully the trip was short and before he knew it, the Saab 340 was approaching the runway at Stornoway. Beneath him, he saw only white clouds and wondered just what sort of day the island was having. Growing up, he remembered dreich days, days when the drizzle seemed to be a life constant and you never saw the sun. This was replaced by times of extreme winds and rain that he was sure did not fall from above but came at your face side on, driving into your clothing and seeping through to the skin beneath. That cold, damp feeling as you were buffeted along the street had never left him.

The cloud cover broke abruptly and he looked out of the window to catch a first glimpse of the island. But the aircraft was only a few hundred feet up and he could see the runway out of his window. Surely that wasn't right. The blessed piece of asphalt should be ahead of the aircraft not at the side. His hands gripped the arm rests. Staring wildly, he felt exposed. There was nothing he could do. His life was in the hands of the pilots. He should have come by ferry.

A hand was placed over his and he turned to see Hope saying it was fine. She spoke loudly and he heard something about it being due to the cross winds and that the plane would soon straighten. Her free hand was making a flicking motion to help her explanation but in truth it was the smiling face, delightful scent and wide green eyes that was calming him down. He drunk in her visage as the aircraft made that slight adjustment and landed smoothly. Having landed, he removed his hand and felt embarrassed. He had behaved like some old man. And then the guilt of enjoying her looks struck him. A brazen woman, he silently requested forgiveness from above.

In the small arrivals hall, they were met by PC Smith, on detachment from Inverness who led them to one of the local cars. The drive into town was short and Macleod looked at the overcast sky and light drizzle that was falling. Yes, he remembered these days. No doubt those little fiends, the midges, would be out and about, eating the skin off everyone. For something so small they were ferocious in the damage they did to you. Hope's white skin would be a prime target. Again he found himself thinking of the brazen woman.

The rest of the murder team would be arriving later that day but Macleod was keen to get on with business and insisted on being taken to where the body was found right away. PC Smith advised that they would have to drop by the station and pick up another driver, as he was required elsewhere. On arrival, and after the formal greetings, Macleod insisted on a car and he asked Hope to drive. But when he held the driver's door open for her, she seemed affronted.

"What's wrong? Don't you want to drive? It's just I want to think some things over."

"Sir," replied McGrath, "you don't need to open doors for me. I'm capable of getting about, I have driven before. And on the way up here, you offered me seats, you let me through first, you do minor things for me like I am incapable. You don't need to."

"I'm just being civil, gentlemanly. A man should afford a woman certain courtesies. It's only right that…"

Hope rallied. "Courtesies? You mean I'm weaker. I think

9

I would kick your arse any day. And I don't remember me shitting my pants on the landing today."

She was so coarse. Modern women spoke in such an ugly fashion. "Don't use that tone with me, McGrath. I am your superior."

"Sorry, sir!" Hope stood in defiance, daring him to say more.

He knew he had offended her but really she had no need to take offence, he was only stating the honest truth. When God had made man and woman, she had been made for him and so to protect her and look after her was only reasonable. But these days it seemed women wanted to stand on their own.

"Shall we get on?" asked Macleod.

"Of course," Hope replied. "But kindly cut out the male chauvinistic bollocks. Sir!"

He found himself staring at her, not in anger but in admiration. He was used to quiet women. His mother had been one, strong at raising her family but quiet in the presence of his father. But Hope was the new breed and as he watched her unblinking face and taut shoulders, he found himself more than a little turned on by her attitude. Like a challenge. But that was wrong.

"Okay, McGrath. Let's just try this again, we got work to do."

Chapter 3

As the car drove smoothly along the single track road, Macleod saw the sheep casually lazing about, occasionally breaking into a hurried shuffle as the car got too close for comfort. Hope was cursing at the animals and he decided at some point he would need to rein in her language. There was no need to swear, no possible requirement that could justify the f-word. If she used the Lord's name in vain he would most definitely pull her up for it.

After turning down a small side road, the car wound its way down to the cliff edge and gave the occupants a long view of the loch before them. Taking a look at the quiet expanse of water before them, Hope whistled her appreciation.

"Look at that, sir. Perfect to swim in or what?"

"The waters are cold up here, even colder than Glasgow and you'd be mad to swim in the Clyde for starters. Park up and find me who's running the show."

Hope parked the car just off the track and headed towards the small contingent of police cars up ahead. Macleod followed behind slowly, chewing over the area. Right out in the back of beyond, he thought. They couldn't have killed her in a more remote or lovely a place. If the sun would turn out this area would be hailed as a paradise but then was that not true of all the islands up here. The weather made such a difference to the perception of the place.

As he approached the group of local officers, Hope was walking towards him, accompanied by a tall man in a shirt and tie who held out his hand. He wore wellington boots but was otherwise suitable to be in any office.

"Good morning, sir," said the officer, "it's a bit on the rough side weather wise."

"Thank you, Detective..?"

"Allinson, sir. I hope the flight up was good enough for you." The man smiled somewhat disingenuously and Macleod wondered if Hope had said anything.

"It was fine, just fine. Now fill me in Allinson, what have we got?"

"If you'll come this way, sir, and I'll brief you as we walk. An early morning walker spotted a body off this cliff edge, looking down to sea. It appears to have been washed up onto the rocks and not simply dropped from the top, as there was little trauma to the body except for the throat which was slashed through. Actually it was more ripped apart, not a very clean job." Allinson seemed to involuntarily swallow as he thought about his last statement and Macleod wondered if the man had ever seen a murder before. It was a sad truth that you became dead to far too horrific a scene in this work, well at least that was what you told yourself. Some of the nightmares said different.

"We had to move the body," continued Allinson, "as the tide would have taken it back out into the loch. Members of the local Coastguard and the lifeboat combined to remove the corpse and it is now back at the hospital morgue. Right, here we are."

Macleod approached a cliff edge and taking care not to get too close too quickly, he peered at the rocks below. "So the tide floods right up and over these rocks? Are we thinking the body came from further up the loch, or down?"

Allinson twitched his head on his rather thin neck and curled the edge of his mouth up. "Well, I spoke to the Coastguard station who said their modelling system would struggle in such a confined area as this loch and they put me onto the lifeboat coxswain. He said it would depend on how long she had been in the water. Given the condition of the body, we are thinking less than twelve hours and more like the early morning, so he reckoned the corpse would have been pulled in from the sea end down the loch."

"Are there any piers or jetties further up?" asked Hope, looking in the general direction.

"A couple on the side of the main road but only one more further up from here."

"Do you have a map?" asked Macleod. "I'm getting a bit disorientated."

Allinson pulled out a standard OS map and spread it on the bonnet of the car. "Now sir, you would have left Stornoway and followed this road out and along before turning down this side road. After that, you have come round the end of the loch you see before us and are now on this side. If you continue up the road, you'll see that there is a marked jetty right there."

"Do many people use it?" asked Hope.

"No, it's in bad repair but it is accessible and people will sometimes go there for a bit of quiet."

"Sort out my mind quiet, or hump the daylights out of each other quiet?"

"McGrath, there's no need to be so crude," chastened

13

Macleod.

"The..., eh... two person physical kind," answered Allinson. Macleod caught Hope's bemused look. She clearly didn't even know her crime. That was the trouble these days, the standards of the new generation had sunk too low, far too low.

"Has anyone been up there yet?"

"No, sir. We've been a little maxed out here dealing with the body and trying to seal off this scene. We've also been trying to identify who the victim is and been canvasing doors to identify her."

"And?" requested Macleod.

"The victim is a twenty-one year old female named Sara Hewitt. English girl, counter assistant in town and former lifeguard who recently started her own massage business."

"What sort of massage business?" asked Hope. Allinson looked quizzically at her.

"Detective McGrath means was it a health benefit or simply a knocking shop?" Allinson looked puzzled again.

"Knocking shop," said Hope, "the old name for a brothel. Was she giving them something beyond a soothing pair of hands?"

"I doubt it," said Allinson, "the shop's on one of the main streets."

Macleod turned away and looked up the loch again. "We need to know the story," he said aloud to the world in general. "Where did she float from? Were there any cars about last night?" He scanned the area for domiciles and saw very few, each hidden off the road, barely visible. Turning around and thinking of where he had driven through he remembered the small village they had passed.

"Allinson, the village behind us, you would need to pass through it to get to the jetty further up, yes?"

14

"Aye, sir."

"Good, then have some of our guys ask round the village. Did anyone see anything last night, anyone strange passing through? Probably a couple, maybe more. If there's no car, then she might have come out here with her murderer."

"We should canvas the other side of the loch too, the town side, there's no guarantee that the body came from this remoter side," said Hope.

"True," nodded Macleod. "Take a run up to the pier, McGrath, see if there's any indication of anything there and call me if there is. Allinson, can you go with her or send one of your men up?"

"People, sir," corrected Hope.

"People, indeed, any officer you deem fit, Allinson."

Macleod stood looking around, soaking in the loch and the air, trying to imagine the place at night. It had been an overcast night, so there would have been little light. This place was perfect to get rid of someone. Watching Hope and Allinson get into the car and then drive off towards the pier, he knew he needed more to run down this killer.

"Do you two get on?"

Hope turned to Allinson checking his intent. He seemed genuine enough. "It's our first case together. Macleod's from here and I got dumped on him because his right hand man was in a car crash."

"Hell of a substitute."

Because she was driving, Hope found it hard to turn and gauge the comment but it certainly sounded like a come on. "The best," she replied.

"You can't be used to a place like this, more cut out for the bright lights of the big city I guess. There's not that much

15

happening here. Plenty if you like the outdoor life and that. Plenty of clubs and groups but the social scene isn't the wildest." Allinson was smiling at her and Hope felt his eyes soaking her up. He was kind of cute and she never minded being looked at. She dressed to impress after all so why would you get annoyed when they stared.

"I'm no wild child, I like a little rural, fresh air and country-side."

"Well if you need any help, just holler. Happy to assist one of our colleagues from the south."

"I may just do that but I doubt we'll get any time for a day or two. By the way does the hotel have any facilities, like a gym or that?"

Allinson smiled. "I'm not certain but if it doesn't there's always the leisure centre in town. I tend to get up early and work out, so if you need company then I am available."

Hope laughed internally. She knew she was attractive and probably a little wilder than most men were used to which often made their heads spin. But she wasn't shallow and she didn't just take a come on from everyone and run with it. But if everywhere else was drab at least there was someone to hang out with.

"Are all your side tracks like this," said Hope, "Feels like the road wasn't built for cars."

"Well it's not like these are main routes to anywhere. I'm not sure anyone really uses the pier anymore. I reckon we get some amorous couples down here but no major traffic." Allinson laughed as he spoke, finding the notion of well-maintained roads somewhat amusing. With a generous smile, this ability to laugh at his personal surroundings endeared him to Hope. She had worked with a number of people from Lewis in Glasgow

16

and most didn't like anything derogatory said about their island.

Within a few minutes Hope had pulled the car up on the pier side and the pair exited the vehicle. Separating, they looked down either side of the pier. Hope scrabbled across rocks with tiny little pools of water lying stagnated, left by the receding tide. Something took her back to days of clamouring over similar rocks with her grandfather, and his tales of the sea monsters that lived in each one.

"McGrath, I've got something."

Hope broke off from her daydream and strode across the rocks back to the end of the pier where Allinson was calling from. As she approached, he pointed to the ground, right where the concrete of the pier started to slope downwards towards the water.

"Threads?" queried Hope.

"Yes, threads from a jacket of something. They seem to be close to the colour she was wearing. I guess we should step away now and get forensics up here. Looks like this may have been the place."

"I'll call the boss," said Hope and pressed the button on her mobile. Holding it to her ear she wondered why it was taking so long.

"You'll need to drive back down. Mobile signal is often pretty poor when you are down the lochs. You go and I'll sit here until someone makes it back."

"Thanks," said Hope. "It really is out of the way here. The lack of houses around, the long trek to a pier no one wants to use, and then a slipway that runs into the water. Almost the perfect spot."

"They usually just say quaint or picturesque in the brochures.

But then we don't advertise the place for murder."

Chapter 4

More of the Glasgow team had arrived, including the forensic section, who had taken over the sites where the body had been found and where it had possibly come from. The local constabulary had come up with an ID for the victim and even an address. Sara Hewitt had not been reported missing but word on the street had caused her boyfriend to ring the station while Macleod had been out at the loch. On receiving the information, he had grabbed McGrath and the pair were making their way back to Stornoway, initially to the massage shop Sara had recently opened.

Although there was a buzz in the town, Hope was able to make her way to the shop without any large crowds blocking her way. However, she did note the distant stares from many locals. And no wonder, she thought, I doubt this sort of thing happens much up here. In Glasgow, they'd just be getting on with their shopping.

"They've got the boyfriend at the station," Macleod said to Hope, "but let's have a look round her place first. She's quite the mystery to us at this time and I'd rather get a picture from her belongings than from someone else initially."

Hope nodded. Macleod was right, it was easier to tell what

angle others came from if you could get an understanding of your own about the victim. She followed him into the door of the small shop. The front had proclaimed different forms of spiritual healing and massage but something just didn't seem right as they entered the shop.

The front room was sparse. A table covered with towels was central to the room and there was a small stereo system lurking in the corner. A range of herbal teas sat beside some bottles containing various liquids and there were a few glass tumblers beside fitness water bottles. The whole place seemed confused, half trying to be something deeper and half trying to be a basic gentleman's lounge.

Macleod picked up an A4 hard backed book from a low table and began flicking through it. Hope glanced over his shoulder and noted the names of men with times of appointments and whether they had paid.

"How much does a massage cost these days?" asked Macleod.

"Forty quid, maybe a little more. Why?"

"Two hundred sound right? There's a few men here who must have been getting some very long massages."

"Paid in advance, maybe? A package deal?" volunteered Hope.

"I'm going to have a deeper look at this, McGrath. Have a look round the rest of the place."

Hope nodded and walked through the door at the back of the shop where she found a small ante room and a set of stairs. The dark blue carpet was showing signs of wear and the white wallpaper had that cream tinge to it that spoke of being neglected for too long. The stairs were steep and led through a door at the top to a simple bedsit.

A double bed with its sheets tossed here and there occupied

the corner of the room adjacent to the windows that looked out onto the road. The curtains were new, unlike most of the furniture and did a good job of blocking out the light and any potential peeping toms. On the bed was a white dressing gown which had a silky look and appeared pretty sheer to Hope. Above the bed were posters of women in classy but highly sexualized poses.

Across from the bed there were a small range of cupboards with a sink unit. On top was a microwave and a hotplate with two rings. Opening the cupboards, Hope discovered a fridge that was almost bare. The half cut melon and single bottle of water were the only occupants and even the cupboards were mostly empty except for a few basic pots and pans. Over the cupboards, the wall had a map of the Isle of Lewis, a tourist edition by the look of it, as there were services advertised. At the back of the room was a small door and on opening it, Hope found a shower room with toilet. A hook with towels hanging was on the back of the door and the shower had only a few empty bottles of shower gel and shampoo.

Returning to the main room, Hope searched the cupboards near the shower room and found a range of sportswear and lingerie. The girl must have been a physical animal, she thought. The sports clothes are serious, good quality and as for the lingerie, there seems to be an abnormal amount of deviant and kinky items. Hope tossed the clothes around and found a pair of handcuffs. Further delving found items of a more personal nature but clearly not for solo use.

Suddenly aware of someone behind her, Hope turned round holding a vibrator and saw the look of disgust in Macleod's eyes.

"Did you find anything of use?" he spat.

"Seems she may have been the entertaining type. There's a lot of toys and sexy clothing. And look at the posters above the bed, real mood setters. But it's all done on a budget by the look of it. She's also a sport's freak, or at least a sport's gear collector. This is all good stuff." Hope watched Macleod walk over to the bed and his lips rose into an angry pout. Standing there, he shook his head.

Hope started to open the few drawers she hadn't checked and found a hairdryer and make-up as well as an upmarket range of underwear. There was also a number of small white packets. "Sir," called Hope and Macleod came over.

"Stupid girl," he said. "This sort of life always ends up bad."

"That's a bit harsh, sir. We know nothing about her yet."

"On the contrary, Detective McGrath, we know she liked to entertain the wilder side of men, and probably in a paying capacity. I swear these girls don't know the demons they dig up in men when they do this. Man's a wild animal, McGrath, an uncontrolled rage of emotions. They would do well to live a more sombre and sober lifestyle."

"Doesn't mean she deserved to be murdered."

"No, it doesn't. But never wake the lion. Too often the hand goes into the fire. Even in my own life. Back before I found my way. Too many don't, McGrath, too many don't."

"You were wild. You don't look the type, sir," rounded Hope.

"I'm not proud of being a slave to the demon drink. But I'm the Lord's now, McGrath. Something we should all ponder on."

Hope ignored the direct message and continued her final rummaging. Soon, she stood up and returned to the bedside where Macleod seemed to be growing red in a suppressed rage.

"That's blasphemy, McGrath," her boss announced. "There's

no place for a blessed symbol like that in this place."

Looking at where Macleod's stare was burning a hole in the wall, Hope saw a bare woman, embraced by a man, but with a cross hung around her neck and nestled in her cleavage.

"Well, some people don't see its significance, sir. It's merely a decoration, something to be adorned in. They don't understand its meaning to someone like you."

"No, they don't, McGrath. If only they did." With that Macleod marched out of the room and Hope decided it was time to go.

She had known he was religious, and also from the island, but the image on the wall had really seemed to throw the Inspector. Hope had no grievance against those with a faith, and in fact envied them in some ways as she had never been sure of anything beyond this life. Friends had died and left her wondering but that was as far as it had gone. Just wondering.

Macleod was in the car and Hope spoke briefly to the two officers in uniform guarding the shop before leaving. Sitting down in the driver's seat, she saw Macleod watch her as she went to start the engine.

"Something wrong, sir?"

"No, nothing. I haven't always had the chance to have someone like you working with me. I was just wondering if you would be able to shed some light on this girl's thinking. I don't really get people like this. Why does a woman do this? You said I was harsh up there. Maybe you're right, but for the grace of God go I, and all that. But you're like her."

Hope raised her eyebrows. "I don't sell my body to men for pleasure. What do you mean, I'm like her?"

"You're young. You like the sports and gym and that. You also like to be looked at, at least I assume you do because you tend to show off your figure. You're fast paced, not like me. So what's her bag in all this, what's she getting?"

"Maybe excitement, sir. Definitely money. There was nothing up there except that her clothing was expensive. All show, all image. Even the posters. I wouldn't have any posters around my lover. I want him to be focused on me. But she wanted to set a mood. So there's insecurity there too. She's actually pretty different to me."

"So I see, McGrath."

"I hope so, sir. You may not like my brashness when it comes to clothing and maybe you won't like my openness in forming relationships but I hope you understand I am not someone creating a show because I'm shallow underneath or need something."

Macleod stared at her. "That's really well put, McGrath. You're certainly showing yourself to being a deeper person than I thought. But don't kid yourself, we all need something."

Chapter 5

The short ride to the police station was in silence. Macleod was chewing over what he had seen, especially the ledger book with the large sums of money, large certainly for some mere back rubbing. Sara Hewitt's boyfriend was at the station and distraught so it would be good to interview him now while his guard was down. Invariably in these situations the killer was generally someone well known to the victim and the out of the way but romantic setting for her dispatch could be boyfriend related. Still, an open mind had to be kept.

The station staff were very accommodating and two cups of tea were provided on arrival before they entered the interview room. The room was plain and simple, with the obligatory desk before the interviewee who in this case seemed rather snappily dressed. Macleod recognised some of the latest fashions from Glasgow on the young man who according to records was twenty-three.

Iain Angus MacDonald had been born and bred on the island, or so the desk sergeant had said. His mother was a councillor, something rare enough on the island and quite a local celebrity. Her husband had died some time previous but this had not stopped her local activities and campaigning. The hour was now past seven and Macleod wanted to get this interview over and done with tonight. He had asked the uniformed officers to carry out door to door around the massage shop, see what anyone knew and some of the Glasgow staff were setting up an incident room. This would be a long night.

Macleod and McGrath sat down behind the desk and looked at the young man with his head hung low. Offering a hand across the table, nothing was given in reply and Macleod opened up the conversation.

"I'm DI Macleod and this is DC McGrath, up from Glasgow to investigate this tragic incident. I'd like to thank you for coming in to talk to us, Iain, at what must be a hard time. If you don't mind, could I ask how long you had known Sara?"

The face lifted and two resentful eyes looked back. There had been tears and the young man's face was sagging, pain wrought from every feature.

"Two years. We'd been together two years."

"Did you spend much time at her flat above her shop?" asked Hope.

The man nodded and sniffed. "She's only had it three months. We used to take it in turns stopping at hers or mine. She never liked to be there if she had clients, I don't think she…," -Iain sniffed again – "wanted me around if clients were downstairs. Said it wasn't professional with someone stomping around upstairs. Besides she had no TV. My place was better for a night in."

"So you weren't often at Sara's?" probed Hope.

"Hers was in town, so that was what we used if we had been out. Saturday night at the club and then walk back to hers. Was less than fifteen minutes. I'm out of town and that would be a scramble for the taxi. God, she wore some hot outfits on a Saturday."

Macleod fought to ignore the blasphemy. "Can you tell us a bit about Sara? We've seen her flat and she seemed to like to dress well."

The man rolled back his neck and looked at the ceiling. Sitting in a shirt, he seemed to be sweating despite the room not being particularly hot. His hair was dark but neatly cropped, and Macleod thought he could smell a scent from him. He was certainly well groomed.

"Sara always looked good, real good. She didn't care what people said. She always said that a good looking woman should not be afraid to look sexy and sweet. There was no baggage that this island brings. The guys were jealous seeing her on my arm."

"So your relationship was more physical than platonic?" asked Hope.

"What? We were having a lot of sex and stuff yes. As for the other word, I'm not with you."

"Was there more to the relationship than sex?"

"Of course there bloody was. What sort of a shit question is that to ask? I wasn't just banging her and then pissing off." Iain was shaking his head and staring at Hope as if she had committed the greatest insult. "You're just like my mother, that's all she thought we were about. I'd thought you'd be a bit more understanding rather than this old fart here," he pointed at Macleod, "considering the figure you cut."

Hope went to speak but Macleod cut across her. "This old fart would like to know your whereabouts last night and since then, just to eliminate you from our enquiries you understand. Really don't want to burden you any more than we have to at this time."

"I was at home last night."

"On your own?"

"Yes. Well, Alistair called in at about eight and we had a beer but then he headed off."

"Alistair who?" asked Macleod.

"Alistair Mackenzie, my pal. Lives further down the village."

"That's Back, yes?"

"Aye. I was watching that new series on Netflix, the one about the murders in Edinburgh. You two would probably like it." Macleod raised his eyes. "It was good. Then I went to bed, got up this morning and went into work at the garage. I heard some vibes on the grapevine and couldn't get her on her mobile. So I called your station."

"So you hadn't spoken to her last night?" asked Hope.

MacDonald shook his head. "She did send me a text, just a few."

"How did she sound?"

"Honestly, a wee bit pissed. She also sent me a photo."

"What time was all this?"

"Oh, about eleven." He sniffed. "She used to send me pics like that when she got pissed. Got a whole stack of them. Doesn't seem right looking at them now."

"Can we see this picture?" asked Macleod.

"It's kinda private."

"Mr Macdonald, your girlfriend has died and I need to explore every avenue to find out why. You currently have in your possession a photo that relates to her movements prior to her death so I would like to see it. I don't want to come down heavy handed in your time of grief but my priority is solving the reason for her death. So please, if you would be so kind as to hand over your phone."

The man opposite began to weep again but he placed a hand into his pocket and produced a mobile phone. Handing it to Macleod, he sat back in his chair and looked away from the pair of them.

Opening the phone, Macleod merely stared at it, before handing it to Hope. He clocked her grin as she worked her way into the text section and gave a little intake of breath as the picture was displayed.

The selfie showed a smiling girl devoid of any clothing above her waist. She had an attractive face with long blonde hair and a buxom body. Macleod forced himself to not tut and looked beyond her to the background of the picture. He saw a lochside, he saw water. The date stamp said the time of sending was 23:11.

"We need to take that picture for analysis, Mr MacDonald."

"Bloody hell, you can't parade that everywhere."

"I don't intend to parade it anywhere, Mr MacDonald. I intend to get my team to begin an analysis of the background and identify it so I know where your girlfriend was at eleven minutes after eleven. So kindly allow us access to this one picture and I'll make sure they distribute it within the station with her more exposed parts covered."

MacDonald nodded and handed over the mobile. Macleod handed it to Hope and indicated she should leave the room to sort out the picture and send in another officer. The man opposite him was obviously grieving but Macleod needed answers and he also needed to be sure the grief wasn't brought on by an action of MacDonald's. Just because you kill someone does not mean you do not feel grief.

"You said she had had the flat only three months." MacDonald nodded. "So I assume she was only in the business of being

29

a masseur for three months."

"That's right, she'd had the business going three months but she had been doing the massage and other techniques before that. College course. She was good at it mind. Nothing better than having her hands taking out the tension and knots of the day. Of course I got a more private effort."

"Private?"

"Yeah, I was her man. She didn't wear much when she massaged me. You know. Was really…, oh God, she's…"

Macleod watched the man burst into another bout of sniffing and crying. If he was a liar, he was a damn fine actor. Macleod wasn't looking forward to the next part but it had to be done.

"Did Sara do any extras for customers?"

The man stopped sniffing. His eyes became wild and he stood up from his seat, beginning to clench his fists. "What are you talking about? Extras. You dirty bastard. What the hell is that mean to mean? She just massaged people. Men and women. There was nothing else. There was only me that she did anything special for."

Macleod remained seated and held up a hand, trying to calm down the man opposite. It was in these moments that any bluff was usually let down and so he decided to push the issue. "I was looking through her books and it appears a number of gentleman seemed to pay over the odds for her services. I was just wondering if she…"

"What? Was banging them on the side? Letting them have the whole thing? Massaging special areas? You think she was a slut?" At this MacDonald leaned across the table and drew himself up to the detective, raging in his face. "She was no slut. Me, you got that, me. I was the only one who gave her it. Understand!"

"Sit down," Macleod said quietly. "I said sit down. I need to understand why these men are paying extra money. I doubt the massage justifies these numbers and I need to know what she's at. If it's drugs, it's drugs. If it's looking after their dogs, then it's looking after their dogs. Whatever it is, I need to know because someone killed her for some reason. So anything unusual, I need to know why."

"Okay," said MacDonald, unclenching his fists before pointing his finger at Macleod. "But you understand she was no slut. She told me, she only did that stuff with me."

"Did you buy her the posters above her bed?"

"What posters?"

"Oh nothing, just saw a few posters above her bed. Just wondered." MacDonald looked at him strangely but sat back down and buried his head in his hands. Then he raised his head again.

"Look all Sara had was me, her gym and her massage business. We were thinking about settling down but we needed more. That's why she was working in the shop on odd days."

"What shop?"

"MacLennan's. Little DIY store. She knew nothing about DIY but it paid. Better than her lifeguard job anyway."

"Where was that job? The lifeguard one."

"Here in town at the sports centre."

Macleod thought to himself, *that's two places to check out. I think I'll do a little gym work in the morning. Can pick up the DIY store afterwards.*

There was a knock at the door and Hope entered and handed MacDonald's mobile back to him. The man hardly looked at her and Hope leant in close to whisper to Macleod that MacDonald's mother was waiting outside.

"Mr MacDonald, thank you for your time and candidness. I believe your mother is outside and you've had a rough day, so I intend to stop this interview right now and let you go and rest." Macleod stood up and waited for MacDonald to react. As the man stood up, Macleod put out his hand and shook the man's right hand before thanking him for his assistance.

"My sincerest condolences, Mr MacDonald."

"Just get the bastard that did this, okay."

"I fully intend to. If you will follow me."

Macleod led the man out through the corridor to the front reception area where a middle aged woman sat in a long skirt with leather boots just showing underneath. She wore a green blouse with a flower motif and her auburn hair was tied up behind her. A leather bag was slung over her shoulder and she showed deep concern when MacDonald emerged from behind Macleod.

"Oh Iain, how awful." The woman placed her arms around the man but he showed little to acknowledge her efforts.

"Good evening Madam, I am DI Macleod and behind me is DC McGrath. Are you going to take care of Mr MacDonald, he's had quite a shock?"

"My apologies, Inspector, my name is Marie, Marie Smith, councillor for the Back area. Iain is my son. I'll take care of him. Time to go home, Iain."

Macleod smiled. "Good, he could do with some understanding company. Just for our records would you state your full name. Sorry, just formality."

"But of course, it's Marie Hannah MacDonald-Smith, but I usually just go with Marie Smith since my husband passed on."

"My condolences, Ma'am." Macleod turned to McGrath.

"Did you get that?" A little stunned, Hope grabbed a notebook from her rear pocket and wrote the name down. "Well, thank you again and we will be in touch tomorrow as you would expect."

"Of course Inspector," said the woman and led her son out of the front doors of the station. Macleod lingered at the door watching the pair get into a red car.

"Formality, full name, what was all that about?"

Macleod turned to his partner and sniffed. "It's a hunch but some of those names in the book, I doubt they were real. Most were not island names when big money was involved. However one recurring set of initials were M and S. Or M and M-S. Or MH and S. There were a number of similar initials. I'll need to recheck but I think we may have found a client who paid big money. Now I really can't tell if she was a woman who needed a woman's touch. But tomorrow, if the name's check out, we need to find out."

"Bit much being involved with your son's girlfriend."

"That's families for you. Sometimes I'm glad I didn't have any kids. My wife would have liked them but I've seen too much heartbreak caused by them."

"Well we can't have you being any more miserable."

The comment was quiet, under the breath and not intended for his ears but it stung. Macleod turned but Hope was already walking back through the doors of the reception lobby. Despite all she represented, the turbulence and casualness of youth, he still wanted to be liked by her. His love had been gone twenty years now. And the hunger for someone, some woman to share things with had him all eyes and feelings for any woman who got onto his radar.

Steady, he thought, God will provide, He will provide.

Chapter 6

I t was one in the morning when Hope drove the car into the hotel car park. One of the good things about Stornoway was that you didn't have to travel far to your accommodation. As the Inspector sought someone out to give them their rooms, Hope collapsed in one of the chairs in the lobby area.

Looking around she saw a man asleep at a table in the corner. His shirt was hanging out of his trousers and Hope guessed that there had been some function on in the hotel as he was looking rather smart. Beyond the man, there was a shield and arms on the wall and some rather quaint figurines on a mantelpiece above a fire place. The fire had died down but she imagined it must be a welcome sight in the winter months, especially with the winds and rain they got here.

Macleod returned with two keys and they followed the signs on the walls up a flight of stairs to their respective rooms. The corridors were like that of many hotels, the same basic colour on walls without a pattern which always gave Hope the idea she was in a recurring dream in a maze she could not escape.

"Meet in my room in five minutes for a quick plan for tomorrow. We'll need to be on the go early I think."

Hope nodded. "Mind if I change and come through. I could

really do with getting out of these clothes."

"Of course," said Macleod but he seemed rather abhorred at the idea. "Do you want a drink?"

"Wouldn't mind a whisky, Sir."

"Well, that's a walk to the bar. I don't think there's a mini bar in here. And I don't drink, myself. There's probably tea if you want it."

"Coffee, sir. See you in five." Hope turned the key and opened her door, dragging her case inside. Throwing it onto her bed, she kicked off her boots and quickly pulled off her top and trousers. Her lingerie followed and she then opened her case looking for something suitable to wear in her boss's hotel room. She saw there was a balcony window behind some net curtains on the far wall and walked right up to it, peering through the material to see what the view was from outside. There was a street below and despite how she fancied feeling some cool air on her skin, she reckoned a DC standing in the raw was bound to attract attention from any passers-by. Not a wise career move.

Turning back to her case, she pulled out some pyjama bottoms and her beloved Raiders top, the American football jersey was large on her and had perforated holes as it was the real thing. Despite this it would provide adequate cover. Then she thought of Macleod and how conservative he was. Rummaging again in the case she took her light green dressing gown. It was only knee length but it should show him the correct degree of modesty.

Hope grabbed her notebook and pen and exited her room to stand in front of Macleod's. She knocked gently, trying not to wake up anyone else. There was a small cry of "just a minute" from inside and she stood patiently.

Macleod was going to be a challenge but she knew he was rated by his boss. In a changing police force, he was known to be struggling with the rise of women and with gender issues as a whole but he was also known to be one of the best detectives going. Indeed, he had the sense to only infer prejudices, not speak them outright. And as a devoted churchman, a staunch Presbyterian and not from the moderate churches either, he was certainly no progressive. But if she could impress him, it might help her career.

The door opened and Macleod held it open as Hope walked in. He offered her the seat at the desk but she shook her head and said she would take the bed.

"I know you younger people don't really see any issue but I'd rather you sat on the chair. I'm not that keen on you being so underdressed in here but to be lying on my bed isn't really appropriate."

"I really don't see any issue," said Hope, "and trust me, sir, this isn't underdressed. But as you wish, whatever you are at ease with." She noticed a coffee was already waiting for her at the desk in the room and sat down and took a sip.

"Hmm, that's nice," she remarked trying to break the tension.

"No it's not. It's the same cheap rubbish you get in those wee packets. If we're here for any length of time we'll need to get some proper stuff sorted. Especially at the investigation room. But anyway, tomorrow McGrath. Where should we be looking?"

"We need to check her recent places of employment for any issues. So her job in the shop. Also maybe check the gym, both on an informal and formal fashion."

"Agreed. I think it's open early. I was going to take my run on the treadmill tomorrow morning and see if mouths are talking. If she was the gym addict it looks like then I would expect her to be known there."

"I'll come down too. Gym and the pool, sir, worth checking both."

"Good," said Macleod. "It opens at seven so I'll meet you downstairs. You having breakfast before?"

"No, can't work out on a full stomach."

"Me neither. At last something in common, Hope."

Looking up from her notes she saw him smiling at her. This was obviously his attempt to connect, to make things easier. It was pretty flippant but she smiled back.

"We need to speak to our council woman again. If you were right about the initials, I think it best I take her. You should talk to MacDonald again. We should get to them early tomorrow, right after gym."

"Indeed. And McGrath, if she was a customer, then I think she'll want to keep it quiet, especially if there's sex involved. Being a lesbian won't go down well up here to a lot of people. It's more open than it used to be but it ain't the mainland." Macleod shuffled a little awkwardly on the bed.

"From the look of what photos we have of her, she was a pretty attractive prospect to an older woman. She had a good figure, toned from the gym. And that councillor had shape for her age too. I could see it happening between them."

Macleod was shifting uneasily again. It was obvious the whole lesbian idea was making him uncomfortable despite his probably seeing it many times before in cases back home.

"What's the issue, sir? You seem a little off when I mention the two women possibly being together."

Macleod stood up and walked to his window. "It's like this, Hope. You no doubt know I have a faith in the Lord. He has

37

been with me a long time now and has stood by me when I have struggled. Well, I ain't that sure he approves of women together. But that's me and I don't going around shouting or decrying anyone, because people have a right to their life, whether I believe things are right or wrong." He turned back to her. "I hope this doesn't offend you but you did ask me."

Hope smiled but was wondering where this was going to go.

"When I grew up here, that sort of thing wouldn't have been tolerated. And there are plenty today who wouldn't either. And the papers will have a field day with those who would cry out against and those who stand up for it. I guess I don't want to see the powder keg explode. This place was home, Hope. It was home."

"Isn't it now?"

"No. No it isn't."

He had gone silent, unnervingly so and Hope decided not to push the issue at this time. She stood up and drained her coffee. Macleod was looking out of the window into the night which was almost a twilight rather than true dark.

"In the summer, it is almost light all the way through the night, Hope. Can you believe that? And in the winter it's dark so early. Apparently Shetland's even more extreme. When I was young I used to be out there wandering the town, stumbling along, hammered beyond belief. But I found my salvation in these churches, Hope. It means a lot to me this place, I hate to see it in a scandal, something the papers would relish. You get that?"

His eyes seemed pained when he looked at her with the question. She smiled and nodded. "But things change, sir. Sometimes we have to change with them."

"But what if it's a change for the worse. Do we just jump in the river? Do we simply stand on the bank and watch it flow past? Or do we build a dam and stop it?"

"That sounds like something that's going to piss a lot of people off, building a dam."

Macleod smiled. "Most people argue back. You really have a tender side, McGrath. Now you'd better go to bed, we have an early start."

"Yes, sir." Taking her notebook and pen, Hope made for the door. But something was bugging her, deep in her mind. "Sir, this faith of yours, is it really worth all these questions, this beating yourself up with the rights and wrongs? Why not just be free of it and be open to all things."

Macleod laughed gently. "I should say it's obviously worth it. But I won't just give you the party line. Sometimes I have my doubts, but sometimes it's the only thing that keeps me standing. You'll never have a friend like Him."

"The Genie in Aladdin. He sings something like that. Sorry, that's a bit flippant."

"Maybe. I don't know the song."

Hope said goodnight and exited to the corridor. It had all gotten a bit heavy, way off case. Opening her own door she locked it behind her before throwing the notebook on the table. She peeled off her nightwear and snuggled under the covers. Try as she might she could not sleep, questions about what truly bugged her boss being here ran through her head. But these thoughts had to fight away a little tune sung by a blue genie, which seemed to be on repeat.

Chapter 7

Macleod felt like his legs were going to go from beneath him. The machine kept turning and that cursed black underneath him meant he had to pump his legs lest the track take him off in an embarrassing fall. Around him were the dedicated followers of exercise, all honed and fit and probably laughing their heads off at him. Desperately he managed to grab his water bottle and take a swig on the run. A few minutes later he had had enough.

Taking a seat in the corner - while he was hydrating of course, never from fatigue – he watched his colleague on the cross trainer. She had been sitting in her Lycra outfit with just a fleece on over it when he found her in the hotel lobby that morning. Although a widower after his beloved wife's death, he chastised himself for staring at the woman without engaging her feelings and emotions. Never would he want to say she was an object. But this morning, maybe because of tiredness and a lack of sleep, he could not help but stare at her legs.

And now he was watching her drive herself to the limit on a cross trainer, hair tied up behind her and her body working hard. Come on, he thought to himself, this is work, not pleasure. Nonchalantly, he scanned the room. There were two men lifting weights, both mid-twenties, and Macleod walked up beside them and lifted up a couple of hand held weights. Slowly he raised his arm on either side.

At first the men shot a glance and then they began to speak to each other again.

"Tragic. She was a gorgeous girl too."

"Aye and for something like that to happen here too. Total waste."

"Did she really know what she was getting herself into?"

Suddenly the conversation slipped into Gaelic and this coincided with a glance at Macleod. He never changed his pattern of weight lifting but instead listened passively, showing no emotion as the fluent Gaelic conversation flowed over him.

"Just be careful. I reckon that guy is the detective come up here."

"Yeah, Annie said the Glasgow ones were up for this. Still it's a shame."

"She certainly had the business. Never short of customers."

"Yeah and she had the hands. You ever had a massage from her?"

"No, the missus would have killed me, what with her view of the girl. Did you?"

"Yeah. Bloody magic. Think I had her massage me four or five times. Nothing like having a gorgeous girl like that working your muscles. Mind you, she did more than that."

"So I heard. You ever..."

"No. I didn't. Would have loved to, she looked a good one. Cracking body and boobs."

"Yeah, well, it caught up with her, I reckon. There's always jealousy when you're putting it about."

"Still, real shame. She looked great dancing on a Saturday and those outfits she wore. I reckon she was advertising for the massage parlour."

Both men laughed and then went sheepish, possibly remembering the girl was dead.

Macleod had been there for over a half hour and was actually amazed at how little was being said but then most of the fitness fanatics were very self-focused. Maybe he should move to the cafe and see if anyone was talking there. Looking around for McGrath, he saw she had departed and so grabbed his water bottle and returned to his locker.

Having grabbed his wallet from the locker and a towel to put around his neck, Macleod made his way to the cafe where he ordered a coffee and some fruit in a bowl. A dose of yoghurt was added on top and he took his healthy option to a table all the time remembering the good old days when he could just have fry up after fry up. Cholesterol had seen to that.

The tables looked out through windows to the swimming pool and he scanned the water for a sign of his colleague. She had mentioned a swim but he could not see her. There were a number of individuals all swimming up and down, putting in their lengths before the day began. Macleod closed his eyes and gave thanks for his food. On opening, he found his eyes drawn to the showering area beside the pool and a figure he found familiar.

Hope was standing with her back to him in a red bikini as she let the water run over her. While not obscene, the bottoms were certainly reaching the limit and as she stepped from foot to foot, Macleod could not help but watch her bottom jiggle. Ashamed he turned away to his food but after a spoonful, he found himself staring again. Hope had turned round now and he drunk in the view as any lonely man would.

Her eyes were closed and a bottle was in her hand. The shampoo was placed into an open hand and then she began to wash her hair, eyes closed. He thought it wrong to stare but he continued, mesmerised. Part of him wanted to say "tart" and then look away disgusted at her. But he couldn't. His dealings with her so far made him think of her as a decent person, thoughtful and intelligent. Again he returned to the bowl of fruit.

His mind came back to his long departed wife. She had been fun, vociferous, and always keen to push his limits and that of the way of life up here. And he had put a lid on her, grinding her down, never letting her be free. When she went into the water, he knew he had a part to play in it. Some spirits should not be stamped on.

Looking up again, he saw Hope tying up her hair behind her, her full body face on to him. The male animal in him stirred and he felt dirty looking but couldn't turn away. Even when she looked up and waved, smiling at him, he didn't have the decency to stop. He watched her all the way to the cubicles.

Macleod closed his eyes and asked for forgiveness. These moments were becoming too numerous. He could not stop himself. Someone might say he needed a good woman beside him again. But he would never take such a free spirit again. Instead he would need a quiet, obedient wife. It sounded bloody awful. He mournfully ate his healthy breakfast thinking about a decent fry and a fun woman to cook one for.

Hope appeared before him, dressed in a pair of blue jeans, a tight fitting crop top and an open blouse over it. Her boots were fashionable but practical.

"Find out anything?" asked Macleod.

"Well, she wasn't the most loved character in the world. I overheard a couple of the women talking about her as if she was the reason that all the good men were turned sour. One even said they were glad she was gone. I got the feeling that a few people knew or thought she was doing extracurricular massaging."

"I got the feeling it was well known too," said Macleod "and yet MacDonald acted like it was the most ridiculous revelation ever. It puts a strong thought in my head that whoever killed her did it because of the book and the fact their name was in it. Did you garner anything else?"

"Not really, sir. It was mostly gossip, there was no one talking as if they had first-hand knowledge yet I guess someone here must have."

"You go and meet our councillor as she should be getting in soon. Don't let her know we suspect her name being in the book yet, see how it goes first. We also need to see who else is in that book and that may take a bit of deduction and maybe getting someone to look over the book."

"One thing occurs to me," said Hope, "If she didn't confide her extra activities to her boyfriend maybe she did to someone else."

"Indeed. Good line of thought. But who? We need to keep our eyes open for that." Macleod's eyes strayed back to the swimming pool. He watched a woman with auburn hair step into the showers and then make her way into the pool. "You may not have to go far for your interview, McGrath. It appears your councillor likes her early morning swim."

They both watched the sleek figure swim length after length as they sipped their drinks. The woman seemed to glide with ease through the water, turning in a tumble at each end.

"What age do you think, sir?"

"Mid-forties, although she could be a good looking fifty year old." He watched the councillor get out of the pool. "She

44

certainly has held her figure but then again, a woman in the public eye."

"Or maybe she just looks good. Some people get all the luck. Hope I look that good at her age."

"Well, you've certainly made a good start." It just slipped out and Macleod froze as the words came out. Hope looked somewhat taken aback before a sly grin came across her face. "Sorry, I shouldn't have said that. Very unprofessional. I was just meaning you have that freshness of youth, that glow."

"So it's downhill from here then," teased Hope.

"No. It was just a simple compliment that came out wrong. I apologise if it caused any offence."

"If I took offence at that I might as well go home with the comments I get in this job. I think I'll grab her coming out from the changing rooms see if I can get her off guard. Do you want to join me?"

"No," said Macleod shaking his head, "I'll go see the manager here. Text me when you're done. If I'm finished before you, I'll walk to the station and touch base with the team. I said we'd brief at ten anyway."

"Okay, I'll go do my hair at the hair dryers and catch her coming out."

Macleod watched Hope rise and disappear back towards the entrance to the swimming pool. As she made her way down the corridor he couldn't help but watch her wiggle. Then he bowed his head and asked for forgiveness again. You need to focus, Macleod, he thought, too many other thoughts coming in.

He drank his coffee and then stood up wondering if the manager would be in. Walking along the corridor he spied a woman at reception and made a bee line for her. Apparently the manager would be another twenty minutes but of course he was welcome to wait. She offered coffee but he declined.

From a chair beside the reception, he was able to see through the glass in the doors to the swimming pool. It let everyone see the hair dryers and there were a number of women drying their hair, applying a touch of makeup. There was also a man drying and brushing. Macleod found it hard not to judge for in his day, this sort of preening said something else about the sort of man you were. Probably unfairly. But it was definitely a thing back then, men had their spaces and women their own. These days things seemed to be much more blurred.

He watched Hope brush her hair and realised that she wore hardly any make up, at least none he could tell. He let his eyes focus onto some of the other women but he struggled not to revert back to Hope. In the end he picked up a free paper from the stand next to his chair.

It was the local free ads paper and he saw a story on the front about developments in the harbour. Flicking on through, he saw school news, new restaurants, a review on some album by a band he had not heard of and a recipe for a sponge cake. And a lot of adverts.

Macleod had an eye for detail amidst a lot of words and he quickly spotted the advert for massage therapies. It was simple and clean, and looked like any other advert there. His attention was diverted for a few seconds as he caught Hope walking out of the front entrance with the councillor before he put his head back in the paper.

There was a brief article about Sunday opening deep inside the paper. It was nothing controversial, a simple piece explaining the views of a religious organisation, after all a free ads paper was not going to behave like the scandal rags with these issues. But it reminded him of his time here, when Sunday was a blessed day. Church morning and night, a day of peace unless he was working. Glasgow was not like that, always on the go. He missed that peace now he was in the hurly-burly of city life. But she would have loved Glasgow. Island life drove her insane. Maybe island life had killed her. Actually, there was no maybe.

Chapter 8

Hope fought through the knot in her hair with her brush, all the while keeping the area behind her in sight by staring in the mirror. Having intended to stand there and pretend her hair was giving her trouble, it was not a relief to find that the red headed mop was actually fairly matted. But her target soon drifted into view.

The council woman was wearing a cream blouse with a jacket thrown over it and a figure hugging black skirt that reached to her knees. The legs beneath were made sleeker by her tights, or possibly stockings and ended in a not unreasonable pair of heels. Fashionable but practical. This made Hope smile and she stood her ground, continuing to brush her hair.

There were spaces away from her but the council woman took the mirror beside Hope and began to delve into her bag. A brush was produced and she took hold of the hair dryer on the wall. Working her hair under the blast of invisible heat, the council woman kept glancing at Hope through her mirror. Keeping a straight face, Hope smiled inside and awaited contact.

With her hair sorted, the woman put her brush away, closed up her bag and then pretended to suddenly spot Hope.

"Detective? Is that you? Can I just say how much I appreciated how you treated my son yesterday. It's a God awful situation but you have been so considerate."

"Thank you," said Hope, noticing the woman step closer. "We will need to ask some more questions today, of you as well. If you could pop down to the station this morning?"

"Actually," replied the woman giving a thoughtful look, "it's a busy morning. Would you be free to come over right now to my office? Have you had breakfast? If not I can offer you some over there. I always have plenty around for myself as I never have breakfast at home. No point going back once your workout is done."

"Well, I guess it would move the day on. As you can imagine, there's a lot still to do, that's why I wanted to get in here early."

"Oh indeed. You must join me another morning, I can have company while I work out. It's a funny lot you get in the mornings, more interested in their body rather than the body next to them. Would be good to have different company for a change."

Hope tilted her head feigning a slight blush. "Well, maybe. If there's time. But shall we go to your office then? I am actually getting rather hungry."

"By all means. Follow me and I'll show you where we are. It's just across from here, the rather drab looking building that dominates. I do like those trousers you're wearing. I'm not sure the same pair on me would give such clean curves on my rear."

If a man said that he would be seen as offensive, Hope mused. Yet she can drop that in and always claim it was just a compliment. That was the thing, she thought, when dating women they can say things right away a man is scared to. That's definitely part of the attraction.

Taking the lead through the door, Hope was aware of the eyes on her from behind and as they walked out into the drizzle, she tried to reposition herself so she could see the woman's eyes. Eyes could tell you so much. But you still had to back it up with some solid evidence. Still, it was always a good start.

"So, Mrs Smith, how long have you been a council woman?" asked Hope, as they crossed the car park to the large building with the bland grey walls.

"Please, Marie. If we girls can't talk civilly then we've lost everything. Been three years this time around but I've been active in local life for over twenty years. I'm pretty well known if I do say so myself. Hated by some, hopefully loved by others. That's the joy of being independent."

"No party affiliations. Must be quite freeing, standing on your own platform. And call me Hope."

"Yes, well, you have to stand on your own convictions. And I'm not in this to rise higher, only to serve this place I call home." Marie smiled and Hope noted the pristine teeth.

They travelled through a door and over to a lift taking them to an upper floor. Marie lead the way along identical corridors and only the plaque on the door gave any idea that this was Marie's office. The room was small, almost a large cupboard, Hope thought, but it had photographs of Marie at various shows and gatherings as well as letters, pinned to the wall. There was a large metallic filing cabinet and a coffee machine sat on top.

Hope watched the woman remove her jacket and hang it on the back of the door. Bending over, she reached for some coffee out of the cabinet, unashamed or apologising that in the tight space her rear was right in front of the seated Hope.

After fixing the machine, Marie turned round and sat opposite Hope before producing some croissants from another drawer.

"Sorry, it's a bit rough and ready but I doubt you would have time for a breakfast elsewhere. You can get a decent start in various hotels or cafes but you must be rushed at the moment, so I hope you don't mind this."

"No, it's fine Marie, really. I'm not a girl who needs the high life." Hope pulled her notebook out and saw a look of disappointment on Marie's face. "Sorry, I need to keep this a bit formal, we do have a murder on our hands."

"So it was definitely murder?"

"Is that what the jungle drums are saying?"

"Most definitely, was it?" Marie was leaning forward and her legs were right beside Hope's. The whole position was certainly not that of one being interviewed but rather someone taking charge. Hope sensed a connection being made, an intent beyond being helpful.

"It looks that way but don't let that out. I guess it's no big secret, after all we're up here from Glasgow so it's fairly obvious. Unfortunately your boy is caught up in it, as a potential suspect due to his closeness to the victim. How close were they?"

Marie half grinned. "Not as close as he thought. She was doing a lot of things he didn't know about."

"Really? How do you know?"

"She had a female friend she was really close to. Sleeping with, if you catch my drift. The girl came to me for advice because she was getting into trouble with her rent at her council house. Started asking about how things would differ if she declared her partner, or even got married."

"And this girl is?"

51

Marie stood up and turned to look out through the small window above her cabinet. "You need to keep this discreet. It's not easy for some people being different. You can pay a high price by letting someone know you are gay in some of our communities."

Hope wanted to get a good look at her face but Marie kept her back to her. "It's fine. We won't let anything out."

"It can be worse on local girls. You see the incomers can be written off, ignored as such. But when your whole family is around you here, you can't hide." Marie turned now and Hope thought she caught a look of regret.

"Her name, please."

"Donna Mackenzie. That's her there. In the picture with the guy in the wheelchair. She was always at events, helping out."

"Fairly bland looking considering her partner," suggested Hope.

"Yes but a good soul, Hope. I guess you want to know where to find her. I have an address for her council home. But be careful how you visit, I doubt many, if any, know of her connection. They were very discrete, very private."

"Can you write the address down for me?"

"Of course," said Marie, "My Iain has no idea. He was daft enough to think he was the main one just because she spent every Saturday night out with him and let him in her bed too. But she didn't see her bed as something precious." Marie's eyes wandered slightly as if in thought.

"How do you reach that conclusion?" probed Hope.

"Well, she couldn't have. I heard she entertained a lot. A lot of men flowed through her door. Especially since she started up that damn shop."

Hope sensed an inner pain bubbling to the surface and part of her wanted to let the woman have a moment. But the detective in her pounced for the kill.

"Did you resent that? Did she let a lot of women in?"

"Oh no, a lot of men. She liked it, saw it as fun and a way to make money, I guess. But only a few women."

"But you had to pay. I guess that would hurt knowing you weren't the favoured one."

Marie looked shocked before crumbling and falling forward into Hope. The woman dropped to her knees, her head now snivelling on Hope's lap. She knew what Marie was wanting, for Hope to caress her hair. She didn't trust this whole show but maybe she could learn more. Hope let her hand start to brush Marie's auburn hair.

"Was she wonderful?" asked Hope.

"Yes, yes she was," Marie sniffed. "But she never let me in. Not truly."

"Were you with her that night?"

Marie stopped her weeping and looked up at Hope, her face suddenly sharp. Getting up off her knees, the scowl on her face stayed.

"Get out! Get out of my office."

"Hey, you invited me here. I never asked."

Marie's eyes were alight and Hope could see the anger behind them. She'd gone too far, not been subtle enough. But the woman had exposed a part of her life that was hidden and Hope now knew more. And part of her believed that Marie could have actually have killed Sara Hewitt. Her come on and breakdown may have been an act, although would Hope have known any of this if she had not been forthcoming?

There were too many questions and only a woman with her shutters up in front of her, so it was time to back down.

53

"If you need me, you can contact me." Hope placed a card on the table but Marie's eyes never left Hope's face. "Where were you two nights ago? You'll need to answer this here or at the station. And trust me, you will be making a statement to us."

A measure of calm returned to Marie's face and she turned her back on Hope. "I dined out with the women's league. You can check with them at the church. It's the Church of Scotland down from the station."

"We will. Don't leave town."

Hope turned on her heel and made her way back along the matching corridors until she found the stairwell and exited the building into the continuing drizzle. Sara Hewitt seems to have been a right girl, thought Sara. Clients, boyfriends, girlfriends and lovers all around. This could take some sifting out. And we need to see her true lover.

Today was going to be a busy one and she felt glad she had had her workout. Returning back into the leisure centre she collected her belongings from a locker and then made her way back out into the car park. Then she stopped aware that eyes were on her. Glancing up at the many windows, she could not spot anyone but she calculated where Marie's window would be. Something inside her said she had been there watching.

Pondering developments, Hope looked for the car. The car park was far from full but the car was gone. It looked like Macleod had taken it after all. With a last glance at the council offices, she set off for the police station on foot.

Chapter 9

Macleod stepped into the office of the leisure centre manager and was directed to a seat behind an impressive desk. There were filing cabinets and large box files behind the manager's own chair and the room had the look of dishevelled industry. Having never run a leisure centre, Macleod was unsure of exactly how taxing it was but if this office was anything to go by, the job might make being Prime minister seem like a good option.

The man that sat down opposite him was dressed in a suit, unlike the members of staff he had seen in their tracksuits. The man was lean and certainly not unlikeable and was trying to give a cheery disposition without being too happy for the subject matter in hand.

"Thank you for seeing me so quickly Mr Maclean, I'm sure the news came as a shock to those who worked here."

Maclean shifted uneasily. "I shouldn't say this and certainly in public I won't but actually, no. Having had her as an employee, I can see why she met her end." Macleod raised his eyebrows and the man quickly continued. "Not in the sense of specific people. I'm talking about her general demeanour in life.

"I won't lie to you, I found her a fun and very good looking

55

girl when she started here. But that was when she had just left the school and got her first job. She had that way around men. You liked seeing her and she flirted without being so brazen that you could see her motives."

"Did she have motives?" asked Macleod.

"Oh yes. With me and here in the job, she just wanted to get more money, lift herself up. But I don't think she understood that even if I was so inclined, and I wasn't, it's not that easy to just give people promotion."

"What did she do exactly?"

The man shifted uneasily in his seat. "You need to promise me to keep this within the confines of your investigation. I didn't tell my wife about it and you can't. I should have at the time but, well, it's a bit late to say now. Would seem suspicious to her. But you need to know just what Sara was like."

"Okay, I understand how to keep things quiet."

The man stood and took off his jacket. Macleod noticed he was beginning to sweat a little and this was obviously a tricky revelation.

"In the first few months of her employ as a lifeguard, she suggested to me that maybe the health suite we have could be opened an hour beyond closing for use by the staff. I saw nothing sinister and when I checked on the practicalities I thought it a good idea. There's not a large number of perks but this would be one and probably a good team bonding one.

"Well the first few weeks it went well and although I had only announced it as a trial period, I did think it was a runner. In fact I had heaped praise on Sara for suggesting it."

"So what changed?" asked Macleod.

"Well, things got a bit too uncomfortable. She started flirting more with me. Nothing too over the top and usually on a one to one basis. In front of everyone else she was a model staff member but when no one was there she would say the odd inappropriate thing. Nothing too sensational but little come-ons. I didn't react to them, although I probably blushed. In truth, I enjoyed the attention, home life was a little rough then.

"But it came to a head when I went to the health suite after work when I thought it was empty. I had had a busy day and wanted a soak in the Jacuzzi. I'm in there and all is fine. Sara then shows up saying everyone else had gone home. This was normal and I had said I would lock up. She then asks if we could talk about her prospects, promotion and that. I was in no mood and told her we'd chat the next day.

"She says, let's talk now. As far as you are from me that's how close she was to me. And she basically just stripped the lot off."

"What did you do?"

"I just sat there. She was stunning. Young, entering her prime and I was in a little shock. Truth be told, I was in a lot of ways loving it but I knew it wasn't right. I might not be the perfect husband but I am true to my Katie. Eyes may drift at times but I don't let them lead me, Inspector.

"I got up and walked right past her. I guess there's not many days we get put to the test but that was mine. But I also said nothing to no one. Sara never mentioned it either but her come-ons stopped and she started to focus on other men."

"Some of the staff?"

"No. Customers. I caught her openly flirting with quite a few. There was also this one guy who never paid her any attention unless she was off from her duty period. She would always go for a swim when she'd finished and he was prone to turn up after her duty time was up. Almost bang on. Nothing wrong with that but I like to keep tabs on what my staff are doing.

"But then she started disappearing with him into the sauna. With what happened before with myself I decided to check up one night. Sure enough, she was trying it on with him but he wasn't holding back. Caught them in full flow so to speak. I told her to get dressed and waited outside. She came out first and got the full force of my tongue. But he slipped out behind me and he's never been in this place again. Seen him once or twice around the island."

"Could you identify him again?"

"Sure. If I see him I'll ring you, if that's what you want."

"Please do," said Macleod, "Here's my card. Did she stay long after that?"

"No. That's when she started this idea of the massage parlour and sure enough she was out of here within three months. Not sacked. I felt sorry for her to be honest."

"Why?"

"Well, her mother was a bit of an alcoholic and put it about too. Her stepdad, the last one was okay, but the girl was wild in terms of her sexuality. I guess she had no example. But workwise she was great. If she'd leave the men alone, she would have gotten on fine. Her work spoke for itself, she had no need to sell anything else."

Maclean got up and moved towards a kettle on the sideboard. "Coffee, Inspector?"

"Please. Did anyone else here get close to her? Anyone else have the same kind of experience as you?"

"Not that I am aware of," said Maclean flicking the on switch. "Sure she flirted but I didn't hear of any incidents. To be honest I think she targeted those in power."

"It's more common than you think."

"Maybe on the mainland," said Maclean, "but here, we don't get this kind of thing. Not a murder. Sure some domestic stuff, other scandals but not this. I guess it comes to everywhere eventually."

"Sad to say but yes."

Macleod ran through some other lines of enquiry but there was little else the manager could offer. He had seemed a decent man and certainly quite measured in his opinions. The other man was interesting, thought Macleod, especially if something had kicked off properly between them. But what did she gain from him? Macleod counted himself lucky he never had a body he could use as a weapon, all these temptations were far from him.

He walked out into the drizzle and got into the car. He should have been heading straight to the station, and by foot, to do his morning briefing but something was playing on his mind and he needed to go there first. He took the car to a road just out of town and headed down the mainly single track to a car park beneath a line of single wind turbines. Small ones but all neatly arranged. The swish of their blades broke through his memories and he remembered that they had not been here back then.

Walking over the field, squelching through various boggy patches, he came to the edge of some small cliffs that over-looked the entrance to Stornoway harbour. The sea was lapping up against rocks that were below his feet and he could see the mark where high tide would have been. Right there, all those years ago, she had jumped.

The tears rolled down his face as he remembered standing on this cliff. They had tried all day to find her. Their faces as he watched them come back to the harbour, the crew of the lifeboat, dejected and exhausted.

Macleod sniffed. Here on his own, and only here did he ever show his anger. Where was your bloody ineffable plan in all this? His heart shook a metaphorical fist at the Creator and he turned away. He knew how families felt at the pointlessness of death. That's why he drove so hard for answers.

His mobile interrupted him. "Macleod," he announced, answering it.

"McGrath here. I thought we were briefing everyone this morning. And where are you with the car?"

"McGrath, I'll be there presently. I want briefed on your morning before we talk to everyone. I'll be ten minutes. And get scenes of crimes to talk to you before we brief everyone too. I think we have quite a girl on our hands."

"I agree," said McGrath. She sounded ominous and he wondered what else Sara Hewitt could have been getting up to.

"Ten minutes." He closed the call. Turning back to the sea, he watched the waves roll up and down, and he could see a head bobbing, a head that looked peaceful, accepting of its fate. He had never comprehended how she could have been so at ease doing it when he was right there, watching. It was the only thing in his life he had ever hated his wife for.

Chapter 10

Macleod entered the room his team had taken over at the police station and made instantly for the kettle. Having just left McGrath with the job of running the briefing, he was giving her a little private time to prepare. He had never enjoyed running briefings and had taken on board his predecessor's advice and got his junior to do it. It had been dumped on him enough times in the past.

As the kettle boiled, he looked around the room. Different police officers were heads down at computers or reading reports. The windows had their blinds pulled and the greyness of the day meant that the lights were required even at this hour. Lewis summers could be like a winter sometimes.

Actually, that wasn't true. May was usually a better month up here than June or July. Similarly, September was often better than August. His favourite was when the north or north-easterly winds came in January and February as the days would be cold but clear. With a decent coat, you could walk until your heart was content up through the grounds of the castle and along some of the coast. You might even get a little snow.

He heard the flick of the kettle switch and realised he had still to put any instant coffee into his cup. Seeing Hope walk through the door, he asked with his hands if she wanted anything. She shook her head and walked to the front of the room. Macleod watched her attend to one of the mobile boards in the room, placing photographs onto it, some with faces, some with excerpts from the book in the massage parlour. As he finished stirring his coffee, he heard Hope bringing the room to order.

"Morning everyone. Thank you for your efforts so far but we have just begun. There's been a lot of footwork done but there's more coming so let's get cracking." Hope grabbed a bottle of water Macleod had not seen and greedily gulped down a swig.

"Sara Hewitt," she continued, "throat cut on a pier up from the place where her body was discovered. There is no doubt she was murdered and not by someone professional. Forensics say it was a kitchen knife, serrated edge, similar to that in many kitchens. She would have had to have been held whilst it took place and that she was likely to have struggled whilst dying. So more than one perpetrator is not unreasonable but there's no evidence to say there is definitely more than one.

"Sara, from investigations, ran a massage parlour and something more. Although it seems she had genuine massage clients, some of her clients were taken upstairs for extras. The book where she recorded her clients has a number of details. She recorded every client that came to her shop so there are plenty of names. DC McKinley will organise you all into teams to track down these names. Most are written in full. We believe these are the people who just got a massage. Those who got into her pants are written in abbreviations, or code."

Macleod shook his head. *Into her pants. She was quite crass.*

"Check up on their kitchen knives as a matter of course and their whereabouts. We are currently working on who were the lucky few to bed Sara and we need to get to them fast. Her boyfriend, Iain MacDonald, says he was unaware of the clients going upstairs for extras. However, he doesn't have an alibi. His mother Councillor Smith has also admitted to being one of the extras crowd. With where we are make sure we keep information like this tight.

"Sara also had a girlfriend, Donna Mackenzie and possibly the true light of her life. The boss and I will be going to see her presently. We have a team tracing bank receipts on Sara's business but no doubt the extras crowd paid cash. Sara also had a stepdad, her mother's deceased, so we'll be looking at him for information too.

"We continue with the stopping of cars near the murder location and we are going to do a canvas in town as well. Also kitchen knife purchases locally, we try to trace those to tie to anyone in the book.

"That's it from me. Boss?"

Macleod stepped forward and looked at the expectant faces. He needed to give a pep talk, stir up the troops but inside he was struggling. The island was bringing back a lot of memories of which only some were good. Seeing the place again this morning, he was starting to feel a permanent chill.

"Thank you, McGrath. Keep on it because someone knows something. Men, and women, who are paying for this sort of thing will often boast and pass it on to their friends how good an experience a girl like this was. Sara Hewitt seems to have tried to get on in life using her sexual powers, and there's no denying she had them.

"But she's dead. So someone was worried, someone was panicking that their dirty little secret was coming out. We need those secrets, we need the dirt. Don't be afraid to push.

This place is like any other. People have secrets and want them kept down. The carpet needs cleaning and we will have to pick it up and give it a good beating to get the dust out. Okay, go to it."

Macleod wondered how many of the people before him realised that people used to beat carpets to remove dust. Still, none of them flinched. Macleod met McGrath in the car park ten minutes later.

"You have the address?" he asked as she approached the car.

"Yes, here."

Macleod took hold of the piece of paper she was offering and scanned it. Marybank, a sort of township on the edge of Stornoway. Never sure if the word village that was used by everyone about these different areas was correct, Macleod had taken to the word township, a term he picked up from a trip to South Africa. A lot of the villages on Lewis were spread out with crofts on the rear of houses causing a greater separation between the buildings. Marybank was a sort of combination of classic village and township. The address he was looking at was at the rear of the village.

The car took its way out of Stornoway town centre to the north of the town. After passing the hospital, it was not long before they had cut into more open moorland and found a small rundown house with drab grey walls but bright curtains in the windows. The car was parked at the top of a steep drive and together the pair of detectives approached the front door. Macleod looked for a door bell but instead ended up knocking the door hard with his fist.

Waiting a few seconds, Macleod rapped again when no answer was forthcoming. Again there was nothing. He tried the door handle and found the door to be open, a trait not unusual in Lewis.

"Police! Anyone home, this is a routine call. This is the Police, anyone there." He stepped inside the front door and was greeted by a bright carpet and a hallway that was plastered with pictures taken from a home printer. Glancing at them, he quickly noted most were of Sara Hewitt and the woman they were looking for. He waved McGrath in behind him.

Again he let out a call for anyone inside but got no response. With a silent hand, he sent McGrath up the stairs that were before him and he took the door to his left. It led into a cosy living room with a stove that still had heat coming from it. There was a blue sofa with a small coffee table before it on which sat a single mug of coffee. Macleod could see the steam still rising from it.

Quietly, he made his way back to the hall and took the next door. The small kitchen looked drab and was only spiced up by the addition of yet more photographs. There was little room to move about and the space was also eaten up further by the clothes horse stood in the middle of the space. An array of underwear, tops and trousers hung from it, all belonging to a woman from the look of them. Macleod wondered where she could be. Maybe she was hiding upstairs.

The blow to his head came from behind and as it drove him to his knees and into the clothes horse, he realised someone had been at the back door of the kitchen which he had not seen properly due to the space constraint. Tumbling to the floor he saw a frying pan, a heavy duty one, fall to the ground beside him. And then there was footsteps, fast and disappearing.

"McGrath!" he called out in pain. "McGrath!"

He heard her come running down the stairs and then into the kitchen.

"Sir? What the hell hap..?"

"Out the door. She went out the front door. Go!" McGrath did not hang about but turned straight away. Groggily, Macleod struggled to his feet and tried to follow but his head was swimming and he clattered into the wall as he tried to move forward. He became aware that he was still entangled in clothes and his feet seemed stuck to them. Dropping back to his knees, he tried to focus but his head rang with pain.

After a minute he raised his hand to the back of his head and when the hand returned he saw red. The blow had been a good one but he was still surprised he had been cut rather than just bruised. Again he tried to get up but realised the pointlessness of his efforts when his legs yielded again.

McGrath returned a few moments later out of breath and red in the cheeks. "Sorry sir, I never even saw her. I tried checking the area but she's probably cut through the back of another house or down a drive."

"Okay, but call it in and get people on the lookout for her. She can't go far in a place like this without someone knowing where she is."

"What the hell? She's pasted you good. We're going to need to get you to the hospital, that's bleeding, and fairly badly. I'll get the first aid kit."

Before he could object, McGrath was gone. Macleod felt useless. They entered the house of a woman, and not a physically strong one judging by her pictures, yet here he was lying on her floor having been battered by her. This was not how he imagined himself. Maybe he would get knocked down by large thugs or criminals but not young girls.

Returning, McGrath dropped a first aid kit beside him and donned some surgical gloves. She then took a large pad and placed it on to his head before arranging strapping around it. She was on her knees in front of him and close up to him meaning her torso was right in Macleod's face. He felt awkward again as this was no position for them to be in but he could do nothing. At least McGrath was quick.

After he stood up, leaning on McGrath to steady himself, Macleod indicated they could try for the car. Hobbling along, his eyes swung along the pictures in the hall. There were pictures of Sara on the grass, Sara walking, Sara in a bikini, Sara with a group at the pier, Sara with an older man…

Macleod pulled up suddenly causing McGrath to almost trip. "There. Take a picture of that one, McGrath. And then find that man."

"Okay sir," she replied, and took out her mobile. "Any others?"

"No. Look at the pictures. All Sara or young people on occasion. There are no other older people. Only this man. Why?"

"Okay, I get you, boss. But we need to get you to the hospital and checked out. I'll drop you there and get on with things. But you need to take it easy, she gave you quite the blow. And I'll get SOCO over here too and see what we can find."

They made their way back to the car, a broken three-legged team and set off for the hospital. The drive was only a few minutes and it was no time before they had checked Macleod into Accident & Emergency. Annoyingly there was a queue and they took a seat. A small television in the corner of the room was showing the news channel and Macleod saw a brief image of the island and then the lochside where the murder had taken place.

"Get going McGrath, I'll be alright here. Go see the stepdad."

"Do you think the girl did it?"

"What do you think?"

"Maybe," said Hope, "but she looked pretty small in the pictures to have held Sara. And she also seemed pretty in love."

"Yes, but domestic issues are often a good reason to kill. But she doesn't seem the type. Maybe she was scared. That's why she ran. I want to know who that man is. His being on the wall just seems wrong."

Chapter 11

Hope drove through the moorland, along the main road that cut across the Isle of Lewis. All around was bog, with occasional clumps of bags. Peat cutting apparently, but Hope had really lost interest once they had started talking about running around in bogs. Some things she just was not cut out for.

Her boss had been dropped at the hospital and he was annoyed at her leaving on her own to go to this next call. Well, it was his own fault getting clobbered by a frying pan by a small girl. Not exactly the stuff of heroes. Hope smirked as she drove the harsh bends.

A flash of white caused her to slam on the brakes and the car rolled up just short of a sheep in the road. The animal simply stared at her before trotting off slowly to the edge. Looking around, Hope could not see where the animal had come from and thought about getting out to get some assistance to remove the animal from the roadside. But the drizzle had started again and she had work to do. Shrugging, she opened up the throttle on the car again.

Ness was a decent twenty miles from Stornoway and Hope felt it was tucked away, as far as possible from the main town. As she drove the long road through other villages, she saw how the houses hugged it, crofts lying out behind them and to her left a view of rain clouds dropping their wares in lines to the horizon seemed strangely impressive. But the wind was strong now.

Arriving in Ness, it took a local man to help her find the house in question and she pulled up in front of a small cottage with fading white walls and an overgrown garden. Leaving her jacket, she knocked on the door of the house and then started swearing under her breath. Damn, it was cold, she could have done with her jacket. Come on, come on.

The door opened and a tall man in jeans and a brown jumper looked her up and down. He was clearly enjoying the view as he didn't stop looking or break the silence.

"Mr Smith?"

"Yes, that's me. Who's asking?" replied the man, still looking Hope up and down.

"Detective McGrath."

"Have I done something wrong? Because if I have, you can arrest me anytime."

Hope was taken aback. Surely he must have heard. "I have some bad news, sir. Can we go inside?"

The man's face became less jovial and he pushed back his black hair revealing some grey underneath. Nodding he turned and walked back into his cottage. Hope followed and he led her into the kitchen and pointed to a single wooden chair.

"I'm fine, sir, but you may want to."

"Why? What's wrong?"

"Do you know Sara Hewitt?"

"Of course, she's Carol's daughter. I try to see her every month but it's been a few weeks now."

"I'm afraid to inform you, she's dead, sir."

"Dead? No, she's not. She can't be."

"I'm afraid so, sir. Died in the early hours of yesterday morning. I know this may sound insensitive but where were you at that time, sir?"

"Dead? Where was I? God, you don't think I did it."

Hope held up a hand. "I need to ask. Standard procedure."

"Okay. Well, I was in bed. Right in the other room."

"Can anyone confirm that?"

The man looked out the window to the ocean beyond and simply stared.

"Can anyone confirm that, sir? Sorry to press you."

"No. It's been a while since someone was sharing my bed. Oh God, not Sara. She was like her Mum, in fact more so."

Hope grabbed the thread. "In what way, sir?"

"Bloody gorgeous and a total flirt with it. She knew it too. She used to tease me when she was growing up. That age when they have found they can attract but too young to have the sense not to flaunt it. But dead? How the hell? How?"

"We believe she was murdered."

"God, no. She always played too close to the fire. I warned her. I had seen it up close and she was just insatiable. She loved to tease men. Weird considering her real preference was women."

"You said up close," Hope said, her eyes narrowing, "How close?"

"Very, Detective. We were having a BBQ at her mother's and Carol had popped out to get some charcoal or something. Sara was sunbathing in her bikini and I was just lounging on a chair. And then she starts taking clothing off. And she comes right up to me, propositions me right there."

71

"And?"

The man stood up and snorted. "And what? I damn well slapped her right on the cheek. She freaked and hit me back. Hard too. Started a nose bleed."

"You felt bad about hitting her? What age was she then?"

"Sixteen. But I didn't feel bad at all. I had to, otherwise I might have done something worse, like taken her to bed. She has a power. Sorry, had a power. Shit, dead?"

"Yes, sir. Can I get you a glass of water? Put the kettle on?"

The man nodded and Hope spied the kettle on the kitchen side. Hunting, she located some tea bags and two mugs.

"Sugar? Milk?"

"Yes, two. And yes," replied the man his eyes staring ahead. Hope watched as the kettle heated up and just as it started to boil the man got up and exited the room for a moment. On return, he handed her a picture in a gold frame. "That's them. Carol and Sara. I said they were so alike. Not just in looks but also in mannerisms. Everything."

Staring at the picture, Hope saw two women, one close to forty and the other maybe sixteen. The likeness was uncanny and except for the odd wrinkle and blemish, the two could have been twins, never mind mother and daughter.

"How did Carol die, sir?" It was a crappy time to ask such a question but Hope knew she had to.

"Died in a car accident in Burundi. She had decided to take herself off to Africa without saying as much as goodbye and then she died out there. Got a letter from a tour guide over there saying she had been in a car accident and was burned alive. There was nothing left to send back. In fact they simply buried whatever was left out there."

"How did Sara take it?"

"Badly. I tried to help her but it was like she blamed me. She desperately wanted someone to blame, someone to pay. She moved out when she got her mother's money and started in town. Eventually she bought the massage parlour. But by now she was off the rails. Poor Sara, it was a damn rough life in a lot of ways for her."

Turning away Hope made the tea and let the man sit down again and stare at the photograph. Tears were running down his face and she watched his shoulders shake. If it was an act it was a damn good one.

"So what was your recent relationship with Sara? How did it work?"

The man sniffed and turned to look at Hope. "I'd go over to town and pop in on her. In the early days she wanted nothing to do with me, as if I was to blame for Carol's death. But then it all changed and I could sit with her, or go for a coffee. She had a thing about her Mum though."

"What sort of thing?" asked Hope.

"Said her Mum had let us down. That she had made poor choices. I didn't get that, especially when she was dating some guy and working other men, all the time in love with a girl. But I did what I could for her. And she seemed to tolerate me at least if not warm to me. At least she never came on to me again."

Hope supped on her tea, thinking hard on what Smith had said. "She said her mum had let you down. I know you said that you didn't understand that coming from Sara and her lifestyle but with Sara aside, does that comment make sense? Was there anything untoward with Carol?"

"Carol was the best thing I had. Yes, a flirt but she didn't cheat on me or stray. We were happy and then suddenly she's off to Africa. Guess I'll never find out what made her take that trip."

"Did she work?"

"She did the books for a few people, ex-accountant, you see. And she sold crafts in a shop in town. She made enough to keep going, in fact more than enough. She had that gift with people, the one to engage them and get them sold on an idea or something to buy."

Something bothered Hope. It was not that the man was somehow not genuine, in fact she totally believed what he said. It was just that the story seemed wrong. A flirt like her daughter and yet totally on one man. Sudden holidays.

The vibration of her mobile suddenly broke Hope's train of thought and she took it out. It was her boss calling and she answered it briefly. Macleod was leaving hospital and wanted her to meet him and catch up with what he had missed. She said she would see him in thirty minutes.

"Do you have a picture of Carol I can take with me, Mr Smith?"

"Sure, I'll just fetch one for you." The man made for the next room and Hope looked around the kitchen realising how lonely it was. Everything said single person. The kitchen was immaculate like it had been cleaned over and over. Everything in its place. And all the food stuff she could see was in single portions. The kitchen felt lonely.

Taking the photo from Smith, Hope offered her condolences again and left. As she drove back, she placed a call on her hands free and got through to Allinson. There had been nothing further on locating the girl and the routine door to door and car stopping had yet to reveal anything. As Hope thanked him and was about to end the call, Allinson quickly threw in a question.

"I don't suppose you would like to get some food after work tonight?"

Wow, thought Hope. He was cute but I did not see that coming.

"It's probably going to be a late finish," said Hope, and she swore she could hear a murmur of disappointment. "But the hotel does food, so maybe we could do something. What's your name, anyway?"

"Allinson, I told you at the lochside."

"I mean your first name. I don't eat with people who I am only on surname terms with."

Allinson laughed and Hope knew she had hit the right tone.

"John, I'm John. And you?"

"Hope. I'll see you at the station later, John." Hope ended the call before he could reply and gave herself a sly grin. He was cute, a good body. If he's entertaining then tonight might just be a good one.

Chapter 12

Macleod crunched the iceberg lettuce inside the burger and a piece of raw tomato fell onto his shirt. Taking a handkerchief, he rubbed at it managing to smear it further across his white shirt.

"Here, let me," said Hope, taking the handkerchief and spitting onto it. Grabbing the shirt between her fingers she rubbed hard at it until satisfied she had made an improvement.

Macleod looked down and saw a faint ring and a wet patch on his top and muttered under his breath. The waitress came over with their coffees and took one look at his shirt.

"Jesus, you made a right muck of that."

"I'll thank you not to take the Good Lord's name in vain." Macleod's eyes were like fire, burning brightly and giving off the belief that any interference could lead to someone being burnt. Laying the coffees on the table with a thud, the waitress stormed away.

"Bit harsh," commented Hope.

"Really, McGrath? The one who made all heaven and earth and we just toss his name around like it's a piece of doggy doo. Some things you have to take a stand against."

Hope laughed. "She meant no offence."

"She's from here. She should know better. It's because

76

people don't hold their tongue that there's a need for you and me."

"Hardly. It's because people can't get over things and decide to bump people off that there's a need for you and me. That's the truth of it."

Macleod shook his head. "The world's going to pot. There's no standards these days. You can be whatever you want these days, and some people can't make up their minds, even then. Boys are girls, girls are boys. There's no standards, nothing people can hang on to. Even the church is losing its grounding."

"You don't agree with the new order then, sir? Am I okay being here? I know I was a last minute replacement."

"McGrath, this is no job for a woman. It truly isn't. When I was young, men protected women, we did the dirty jobs, left you free to do the raising of the kids, keep the home running. Now, people do what they want and look at it. You want to do this job, well, I can't stop you and maybe these days that's right. But I take you into an interview room and the guy is sitting there drooling, looking you over. It's not good."

"I'll wear my burka next time."

"Don't go there."

"You really need to get your attitude modernised, sir."

"Look, I don't agree with a lot but I follow policy, I make sure everyone gets equal rights as they say these days. But I am entitled to my opinion. And it's a road to hell."

Macleod watched Hope's face as she seemed to be biting on her lip. Her expression went from someone offended to that of the guest at the party who has just got the joke.

"What's so funny?"

"You're going to love our girl, Sara."

Macleod raised his eyebrows. "Why?"

"When I went to her stepdad he painted some picture. Apparently she propositioned him once while sunbathing. Actually whipped some clothing off and gave him a good view. He slapped her and she resented it. He reckons she has been having plenty of sex deliberately with these men despite being a lesbian at heart."

"I did say, the road to hell. The Lord have mercy." Macleod raised his eyes to the ceiling and muttered something under his breath.

"What was more interesting, was that her mother took off from the stepdad suddenly and went on holiday to Africa, only to die in a road accident in Burundi. The tour operator sent him some sort of confirmation but nobody was able to be recovered and repatriated. Then the daughter cold shoulders him and then later is opening her massage parlour and banging these men."

"Having intercourse, there's no need to be vulgar."

Macleod watched McGrath roll her eyes before continuing. "What I'm getting at is the stepdad put this all down to a reaction to her mother's death. But I reckon there's more to it. It's all very convenient. Something smells fishy."

Standing up, Macleod threw down some money on the table. "Come on. You might have a body too distracting for the interview room but you have the suspicious mind of a policeman."

"Person, sir, person."

* * *

McGrath drove them the short distance to the station and they made their way to the operations room. Checking in with

Allinson, Macleod learned that there had been no sightings of their missing girl. However, stopping of cars on the main road had led to a partial identification of a car in the area that night. It was red and a five door saloon. However no number plate was forthcoming.

Allinson also reported that the bus driver who travelled that route earlier in the evening had taken two young women from town to a stop close by the pier where Sara was believed to be murdered. He could not be sure but Sara may have been one of the women.

"I requested that they bring young Iain back in. We found that photo in the house of Donna Mackenzie and I want to know if Iain has seen that guy about. I'd really rather get hold of Donna to ask her but Allinson's finding it hard to grab her. I mean, there cannot be that many places to go to ground up here, can there?"

"You tell me, sir, you're from here," retorted McGrath.

Sara's boyfriend Iain was not in a good way when they entered the interview room. Sat across the table from them, every time he tried to pick up his coffee in the plastic cup, it was spilling due to a shaky hand.

"Thank you for coming back in Mr MacDonald, I appreciate this is not a good time. Is there anything else I can get you, maybe a cloth for the table?"

Macleod was letting McGrath take the lead and was watching the reactions of Iain MacDonald closely. He had requested Hope to push MacDonald in terms of Sara's close friends, to drive a line that would reveal any threats to Iain's position as her boyfriend. It all seemed to be too much that he knew nothing of her other life.

"In terms of friends, and I mean female friends, did Sara have any?" asked McGrath. Hope was smiling, leaning forward and cut a figure most men would at least be taking a good glance at but MacDonald was nervy, looking here and there.

"Of course. There were friends but no one of note really."

"Could you tell me some names?"

"Well, there was Elaine, Anna, and Tina. They would come out with us on a Saturday sometimes but they are my friends really. Sara didn't mix that well with people. She as always focused on me. We'd be out, talking to each other, making out, maybe dancing and then back to hers."

"So how often did you stay over?" asked Macleod.

"Every Saturday. She was busy and preferred my place to stay. She had always come over to my place until I suggested we use her place in town on a Saturday."

"And you only stayed there on a Saturday?" queried McGrath. Macleod caught her glance towards him.

"Yes! Yes!"

"Anyone else ever stay over with you?"

"No," said MacDonald emphatically and a little aggressively. But then he stopped and seemed to ponder. "There were a few times I woke up in the morning and there was Donna there. I just assumed she had come over in the morning."

"Donna?" asked McGrath, innocently, "Who's Donna?"

"Just this sad girl who hung onto Sara's coat tails. I think she liked to think she was Sara's friend. I only ever saw her twice. But I knew her from growing up."

"How?"

"There's only the one secondary school up here on Lewis, McGrath," interjected Macleod. "As a teenager you soon get to know everyone's name if not in any great depth."

"That's right. She was below me in school but even then she

was a bit weird. Never heard of her having a boyfriend either."

"So you only ever saw her round at Sara's twice. And both times a Sunday morning," clarified Hope.

"Yes. Although the second time was a bit strange. I'd gotten up after midday and went to use the shower. Opened the door and realised it wasn't Sara in there. Apparently Donna had decided to have a wash as she had been out all night. Maybe she had had a row with someone."

"Unusual to have a wash at a friends like that," prompted Macleod.

"Yeah, it was. But like I said, she was a bit weird. I think Sara was just taking care of someone she saw struggling. She never talked about her, so I think she didn't know her that well."

Macleod had to suppress the cry within him that wanted to grab this man by the shoulders and tell him what an idiot he was. But then he caught himself. Maybe this was an act. But like so many times you ask this question, he realised it would have to be a blooming good one.

Catching Hope's eye, he gave a nod. From her jacket pocket, McGrath took out a copy of the photo from the wall of Donna Mackenzie's house. Placing it on the table, she remained silent for a few moments and Macleod saw an anger in young MacDonald's face.

"You know him?" asked McGrath.

"Not know him, but saw him a few times when we were out on a Saturday."

"When?"

"In recent weeks. I think he's one of those street pastors from the church."

"Street pastors?"

"Yeah, they give you God when you are down and out and

pissed. But they do help a lot of people home and that. The Pastors are harmless enough but this guy was quite intense. I know she had seen someone in the church to talk to after her mum died but I don't know who. That was before we had got it on.

"But this guy would stop her on a night out as we went along the street. Come to think of it, he was a lot more aggressive than the Pastors normally are. Insisting she stop. I offered to do him but she said she was handling it. Actually it didn't seem to bother her that much. We would just head into a pub or the club, 'cos he never followed us in there."

"What did he wear when you met?" asked Macleod.

"Was always on the street so he had a coat on, usually done up, and had a hat on, like a flat cap. It was usually as we came past a side street. Thinking about it, he was quite secretive and he never wanted a scene."

"What do you mean a scene?" asked Hope. "Did things ever get angry or ugly?"

"Not with Sara, she just brushed him off, told him to go away. But he got hot under the collar a few times. Like I said, he was aggressive for a street pastor."

MacDonald began to sniff again and yielded little more information of use. Macleod retired from the interview and met up with McGrath in the operations room.

"We need to find this guy and fast," said Macleod.

"Why don't we just trawl the churches and find this street pastor team?" asked Hope.

"I'll go to them. We don't want to be seen as word travels around fast in this place, and at the moment, he doesn't know we are looking for him. I want to catch him unawares, see him before he has a defence up."

"Okay, I'll go see her boss at the hardware shop, I believe she was there in the days before she was killed, see if there's anything else the standard questioning didn't find."

"Good, we'll meet up then tonight at the hotel, go over everything."

Allinson rushed into the room and flagged down Macleod. "Sir, sir, you need to see this. He was holding in his gloved hand, a note written on plain white paper. It read, "Sorry about the pan to the head. Meet me at the memorial drinking fountain in the castle grounds, 3am, alone. It's not safe for me."

Chapter 13

Being a Saturday and close to the start of evening, Hope wanted to catch the owner of the DIY store before he left. Tomorrow was Sunday and Macleod said that everything was going to be a little more awkward during the island's day of rest. With the arrival of the note, their plans had been somewhat rearranged. She had been looking forward to a meal with Allinson, a bit of a laugh and who knows what else. Now that was all on hold for a potential early night to get up at 2am.

Driving into the small car park, the store front reminded Hope of an industrial unit rather than a shop and it seemed to be almost empty. Approaching the door after parking, she stood in front of automatic sliding doors that were refusing to do their job. Hope clocked the opening hours. The store had closed twenty minutes ago. Shit!

There were still lights on inside and she was sure she saw movement. Banging on the door, she heard a cry of "shut" coming from the rear. Despite this, she kept banging and a thin man eventually approached and flicked a switch near the top of the doors. They swept open and he looked at Hope with annoyance.

"Can't you read? We're shut, come back Monday."

"Police," replied Hope, brandishing her credentials which the man studied carefully.

"This will be about Sara then. I'm needing to be out tonight so can we make it quick?"

"I'll be as quick as I can, sir, but I am running a murder investigation."

"Of course, officer. Alan Jones. Come in and we'll go to the office."

The man led Hope through to a back room with a simple desk and a number of filing cabinets. He switched on a kettle before grabbing two cups and looking back at her with a jar of coffee in his hand. Hope nodded and they waited in silence while the kettle boiled. Coffee made, they sat either side of the table.

"According to her boyfriend, Sara was working here," prompted Hope.

"That's correct. In fact she was due to work today. That was her routine on a Saturday. Work here and then that fool of a boyfriend would come over and they would go out. You'd see them on the town together, her with eyes everywhere else and him oblivious to it all. Young men can be so daft."

"What did you make of her?"

The man smiled. "She was a heck of a looker. It was nice having her around and she ran a good front of shop when she was in. As you can imagine I get a lot of tradesmen in here and she was great eye candy for them. I know that sounds a bit sexist but these guys are working hard and then they come in here to be served by a pretty and knowledgeable woman. And a masseur as well." The man rolled his eyes knowingly.

"Did you ever get any trouble here, Alan? Any of the men get out of hand?"

He shook his head. "No. Like I said, these are tradesmen, she's just the girl at the till, nice to look at and maybe have a wee bit of banter with but nothing beyond that. I know some of the customers went to her as a masseur as well since she started."

"Any say they got more than that?" Hope could see the man was uneasy with the question.

"I don't like to speak ill of the girl now she's dead but... I know a few mentioned about it, even tried to say that's why I had her here in store, to get extras but there's no truth in that."

"She ever offer anything to you like that?"

"No, officer, and I wasn't looking for it either. I'm happily married. She was an employee, first and foremost. The fact she looked great was a bonus but that was where my involvement and interest stopped."

"Can I ask your whereabouts on Thursday night into Friday morning? Just routine, sir."

"Sure. Thursday was my art class, at the arts centre, seven to nine. Picked up by the wife and then we had a glass of wine at home and went to bed. Left home about eight and came here. Place was open at half past. Stephen, out there, was in here then too."

"Have you many employees here?" asked Hope.

"As you can see we are not that big, so there's myself, my wife also helps out from time to time, Stephen and we had Sara. Going to need someone else now, actually. It's a real shame as I genuinely liked her despite the rumours you hear. Might have been her mother dying that sent her down that path. She worked here too before Sara. That's why I gave her the job really. They were really quite alike."

Hope looked out through the office window to the shop

beyond. She saw a young man of over six foot, with arms that resembled tree trunks. "Is that Stephen?"

"Yes," replied Alan, "Not the brightest but a keen worker. He's been quite sullen today as we all have been with this business."

"Call him in here please."

Alan got up and walked to the door calling the man before returning to his seat. Soon, the tall, strapping young man walked in and smiled when he saw Hope sat there. Although his boss started talking to him, he continued with his eyes on Hope giving a dull leer.

"This is Detective McGrath, Stephen." The man had bolted. The door banged shut behind him and Hope was on her feet in no time. Pulling the door open, she saw him disappear behind some racks of paint. She rounded the end of the rack but he was gone again, now through the aisle of power drills, pulling some to the floor.

"Stop, police. I only want to talk to you."

Hope's command was ignored and long planks of wood were dropped before her, slowing her pursuit. Realising that she was not able to simply catch up with him, she doubled back, keeping low and tried to anticipate the man's movements. He had a choice of two directions at the end of the aisle he was on, so she double backed to cut off one of them. Keeping low, Hope was sure he would struggle to see her and then he came round the corner straight into her path.

Panic filled the man's eyes and he took a swing at Hope which she ducked. Reaching for his other arm, she tried to take it behind him but he was too strong. With an almost casual flick he pushed her into the racking and she cracked her head off an edge. Despite the pain, Hope leapt back as the man ran off catching his ankles with a flailing arm sending him to the ground. He rose slowly, allowing Hope to jump on his back and take him to ground once more. She grabbed a wrist and slapped a pair of handcuffs on to it before attaching them to the other wrist.

"Stephen, what the hell are you doing?"

"She said it was okay. She let me. She offered. It wasn't me."

"Wasn't you who did what?" shouted Hope.

"I didn't kill her. It was my birthday."

"Right, mister," said Hope, "we are going to get up and go back to the office. You are going to sit down and tell me all about it. Up!"

The man did not resist and got to his feet, allowing himself to be led back to the office like a lamb. Hope took him to the seat his boss had occupied. As she was about to sit down herself, Alan asked to speak to her outside. She agreed and closed the office door keeping her eyes on Stephen through the glass.

"Before you jump to conclusions, you should know that Stephen does have learning issues. He's able to hold conversations and but he makes attachments sometimes more than they are. He has a different reality going on in his head sometimes. He's very clever in a lot of ways but socially inept. I don't think he's ever had a girlfriend, not sure if he is really capable. Just so you know."

"Okay. Does he have a responsible adult or anything? I'll need to take him in, given what he's said."

"Sure officer. I think his mum is his official carer, or whatever the term is. Would you like me to accompany you until you can get her? This will all be a mistake I'm sure."

"I'd really like to think so, for his sake," said Hope.

Twenty minutes later, Hope was back in the station getting

ready to interview Stephen. Macleod was out chasing down street pastors and until she was sure Stephen had actually done anything she was not going to call him back. Instead, Allinson would have to come in with her when Stephen's mother arrived.

"You want me to assist or just sit there fat, dumb and happy?" asked Allinson handing Hope a coffee.

"I'll take the lead but I doubt you can do fat."

"But dumb and happy, I'm fine with?"

"Hey, happy's a good thing."

"And dumb?" asked Allinson.

"You probably don't even realise." With that she swept by him, hoping his eyes were still on her. Allinson was just shy of six feet, slightly shorter than Hope but he was attractive and now she was getting tired, as ever, she felt lonelier. Maybe there would be time tonight if she made it.

Once Stephen's mother had arrived with a lawyer, they all gathered in an interview room and Hope gathered her thoughts.

"Stephen, Mr Jones mentioned Sara at the DIY shop and you ran from me. You then said that she let you do it and that it was your birthday. And that you didn't kill her. What did she let you do?"

Stephen looked at his mother who was a woman in her sixties and wearing a conservative dress. Her face was full of worry and her eyes were welling up but she nodded at Stephen as her hands trembled, presumably fearing what revelation would come.

"She said it was okay?"

"Okay Stephen, why don't you just take us through it slowly?" asked Hope.

"I didn't kill her. I didn't do that."

"Stephen, listen to me," said Allinson. His tone was smooth and soothing and his eyes fixed on Stephen. As the man looked up at him, he caught his eye and held it. "Your birthday, tell me what happened on your birthday. Did you get a treat?"

Stephen nodded. "Sara said it was okay. She said it was what men liked, what men wanted."

"Did you want it, Stephen?"

"Yes." Stephen looked awkwardly at his mother. "I went to her shop like she told me to do. I was meant to be in my room working on my model but Mum was out. She took me upstairs. There were pictures of women on the wall."

"Okay Stephen, and what happened then?"

Stephen went red and started looking away from his mother. "We took our clothes off and we…, we…, did the thing."

"Okay Stephen, and what happened then."

Stephen started to sniff and well up. "We met her friend and we took a bus out to a loch. It was still bright and we had some wine. Her friend was nice, she made me laugh."

"What was her friend like, Stephen?"

"She was nice but not like Sara. Sara was beautiful." He bent over as if ashamed. "Especially upstairs where the posters were."

"Okay, Stephen, it's okay. But out at the loch, what happened?"

"I told you. We had wine, and we laughed. We were silly and went for a paddle."

"And then what?"

"It began to get darker. And Sara got a lot of calls on her phone. She got quite angry too. She said she had to meet someone. Her friend took me to the bus and I came home.

They gave me wine as a present. Red wine. It was tasty."

"Did you see her after that?"

"No. I heard she was dead when I went to work. But it wasn't me. You don't do the thing and then die. You don't, you don't…" He broke into a flood of tears.

"Thank God," said his mother and reached over taking him in her arms as he snorted and cried.

Twenty minutes later, Hope was standing with Stephen's mother and their lawyer outside the interview room. The woman looked drained and was so much smaller than her son.

"We have to check out his story but I'm happy to let him go as long as he stays at home. He may know more and if he says anything of note please contact me. Hope handed over her card. "I take it he has never had sex before this point."

"No," said his mother shaking her head, "I wasn't even sure he could. Maybe he's been too sheltered but after his father ran off, it was just hard enough to cope never mind educate him in those things. And he never seemed interested."

"Okay, well, look after him and we will be in touch."

"Any news from the boss," asked Hope turning to Allinson.

"Yeah he wants to meet you at the hotel. Guess dinner is definitely scuppered then."

"Dinner yes, but not everything." Hope slipped a hand briefly into his before walking off. She didn't miss the grin he fought to hide.

Chapter 14

Macleod walked his way through the town streets remembering days when they had done this together. She had liked their walks, holding his hand, constantly telling him all about what had happened. Well, at first it had been like that, before she had become more morose, more stunted by the place.

Turning a corner, he saw the church with its steeple rising up. Church life had been different here and he wondered if it was the same today. Back then, in the country church they had gone to, they would sit in silence before the start of the service, that clock thundering out the seconds as if you were in an abandoned clockmakers.

It was not that they had not had any friends but rather that you had to conform to a certain fit. Hats for the women on a Sunday. She had worn a hat even though she hated them but then she had refused. Macleod had not stopped her but the talk when she consistently refused to wear one had been oppressive. And then there were the words aside.

The hat was a minor thing but there had been so many minor things before a lot of the women stopped talking to his wife. And that was the blow, the isolation, the thing that started her into the depression. And although this was not the church that he had been part of, the mere sight of the denomination name brought it all back. An anger was building in him and had been since he had stepped off the aeroplane. And it was continuing to grow. Looking to the sky, he raised an invisible fist to heaven.

But there was a killer to find and he had not expected to be searching here. At least not for a deliberate killing. Street pastors as well, that was a new one up here. He had heard of them in bigger cities, especially places like America with their gangs. Apparently there had been some great work done and the redemption of souls as well.

Approaching the church building, he saw a light on at the rear of the building and proceeded to the door. Knocking it, he received no response and so pushed at it gently. The door swung open and Macleod stepped inside to a rather dark hallway that led to another set of double doors. Inside he could hear voices in prayer.

Having been brought up in a small country Presbyterian Church, he was used to men standing to pray, everything done in a civilised fashion. But the voice praying now was a woman and around her were voices crying out every now and then to God. This type of prayer was not new to Macleod, for he had seen and heard it in Glasgow but he had not expected to find it here.

Cautiously, so as not to cause the door to squeak or bang, he opened it and stepped inside. The hall was adorned with pictures from a Sunday school or some other sort of kid's group. Chairs sat around the edge of the hall and in a circle standing on the wooden floor were some ten individuals, praying.

Watching the woman before him, her eyes closed and hands

upraised, he thought of his wife. She was passionate about her faith, always praying with such fervour in their prayer times together. But when at the prayer meetings she had sat silent, the tradition keeping her quiet. Or was it? Maybe they were meant to be silent in the meetings. Maybe it was a man's place to lead. However seeing this woman with her dark hair swinging as she almost jumped as she prayed, made him question that premise. Her hunger for God was swaying him into a more liberal stance.

It was another ten minutes before they finished their prayers, with contributions coming in from most of the circle, many short and sweet but all given with energy. As they opened their eyes, a sudden murmur erupted at the man standing just inside the door and Macleod stepped forward to introduce himself.

"Detective Inspector Macleod, ladies and gentlemen, I was hoping to talk to your group leader."

A small elderly woman stepped forward, dressed in a skirt, blouse and cardigan and some stout black shoes. Her hair was grey and had that thin quality of aging, the hair having lost the exuberance it had in its youth.

"Good evening, Inspector, Geraldine Pickering, I lead this group. I'm happy to offer you what assistance I can but if we can be brief that would be appreciated as we are about to go on patrol." The body may have looked frail but the voice was as strong as his own.

"I shall do my best not to delay you." Macleod removed a photograph from his pocket. "Do you know this man?"

"I don't believe so, Inspector but if you want to show it to the rest of the group, maybe that would yield a result."

Macleod nodded and the lady called over her people. One

by one they looked and shook their head until a young girl simply stared. The girl was only a teen, towards the later end of her teenage years but small in frame. Wearing a hoodie, her blonde hair barely showed and her jeans and black jacket gave off that dispassionate air he had encountered so often from the younger generation.

"Do you recognise him?" asked Macleod.

"I don't know," replied the girl in a voice so quiet, she could barely be heard.

Macleod hated this kind of witness. Either say yes or no. Surely people must know. Looking at the girl, he tried to size up if she was genuine or just seeking attention. Given her reticence and the fact that she looked like a hermit crab in her hoodie gave him the impression that she was telling the truth.

"Okay. I need you to concentrate. This is important and I need for you to be as accurate as possible. Where do you think you have seen him?"

"Out here. On the street. Maybe a month ago." The girl chewed in between words making Macleod grind his teeth but he kept up the focus on the photograph.

"Someone else told us that he was a street pastor, which is why I'm here. But I'm guessing he isn't one."

"He certainly hasn't darkened our door, Inspector," said Geraldine. "Anna, think again and tell the Inspector everything you can."

"He was creepy. We were prayer walking and it was raining. My head was down and I was trying to catch up with Iain who had popped inside the hall for a whizz."

"A whizz?" asked Macleod.

"A slash," answered Anna.

"The toilet, Inspector," said Geraldine. "Go on Anna."

"Well, I felt a hand grab my shoulder and spin me round. As he did it, he said he wanted me. It was so creepy as he said it in a sexual sense, like he was expecting something from me. Then he said I had no right to stop. And then he pushed my hood back."

Geraldine placed a hand on Anna's shoulder. "You should have said."

Anna shook her head. "He then realised I wasn't who he wanted. And he turned and disappeared up the side street."

"Did he say anything else?"

Anna looked at Geraldine almost apologetically. "Only *shit*."

"Okay," said Macleod, "so you had a brief look at him. Is this definitely him?"

"I can't be sure. I believe so."

"What was he wearing?"

"A long coat," said the girl almost shivering. "And a cap. With the rain and the dark, it made it quite difficult to see well but I reckon that's him."

"And you said it felt sexual."

"Very much," said Anna. "For a moment I felt like he was going to grab me in other ways but then he recognised I wasn't the girl he wanted. I put it down to him being pissed."

"And was he? Did you smell any drink on him?"

"No, come to think of it, I didn't." She started to shake and Macleod could see the cogs in her mind starting to put pieces together.

"You're here for the murder, aren't you? He could have… I could have been…" The girl began to weep and Geraldine put an arm around her. Macleod wondered just what to do as he couldn't talk about the case itself, couldn't offer a full explanation.

"Anna, I will need you to come down to the station tomorrow and make a full statement to the effect of what you have just told me. I also think you should talk this through with someone trained in counselling. We can get details for you. But you'll have to trust me when I say, you were not his target and I doubt you were in any real danger despite this very unpleasant experience. You said yourself he was looking for someone else."

"Do you pray, Inspector?" asked Geraldine.

"Yes, madam, I do."

"Then please join us as we pray for Anna." With that Geraldine bowed her head and began to speak out loud, invoking her God's assistance. Macleod bowed his head and listened to the old woman asking for the girl's peace and cleansing from this horrible incident. As the woman prayed, he felt a warmth inside, like a presence was with him. It reminded him of when he prayed with his wife. Standing there in this mundane hall, he fought between the joy of feeling this precious experience that mirrored that which he had with his wife, and the pain that every memory of her brought, knowing what he had lost.

"Thank you, Inspector," said Geraldine when the prayer had finished, "I'll make sure Anna gets down to you tomorrow."

"You should really let her parents know."

"I will but she is eighteen. And she's also my grand-daughter."

Macleod nodded. "I'm sorry for your experience, Anna, but you've been a great help. Thank you all for your time."

As he left the building, Macleod felt that same warm glow inside. He looked at the street opposite that would take him back to the station. Surely there would be no harm in taking a longer route back. He turned the opposite direction and headed towards the car park and the harbour. On arrival, he found the car park almost full and people were moving about towards whatever evening entertainment they sought. Macleod ignored them all and stood at the barriers on the far side of the car park, looking down at the harbour water as it splashed up against the retaining wall.

She had been so vibrant. If only she'd had the chance like Geraldine, she could have prayed like that. She did in front of him. She was freer in everything when they were alone. He missed her. All of her. He had held it all tight within, his loss, his pain, his anger. All because she was the one who had been able to unzip his baggage. And now when his pain was at his greatest, she was no longer around.

The water splashed again below him and he watched the froth splatter and then fall back along rocks. It was soothing being by the sea again. And yet it had also brought back the pain. Part of him thought he could stay here forever tossed about in his lonely vessel. But he was a detective and this was solving nothing.

Chapter 15

Macleod was surprised to see Allinson in the hotel lobby. A message from McGrath had told him she had already left the station and that she would meet at the hotel as he had previously requested. *Allinson is still in his suit and tie, so at least he's here to work*, thought Macleod.

"Evening sir," said Allinson, "Hope's gone up for a shower. She said I should wait for you and then go up for the briefing. Said it best if I joined you, if you don't mind of course, just to keep me informed about everything."

"Of course," said Macleod, "I'm sure Detective McGrath is correct in her logic." Brushing past the man, Macleod asked for his key at the reception desk. "Well, follow me, Allinson. I've had a long day and it isn't finished yet."

He did not wait for an answer and strode off to the stairs that lead to his floor. He could hear Allinson following but did not turn round until he got to his room. Opening the door with his key card, Macleod let Allinson in and pointed to the small kettle.

"I'll get McGrath. Make yourself useful, Allinson and put the kettle on. We'll need a cup from McGrath's."

Letting the door close, he took the three steps to McGrath's door and knocked loudly as he could hear the shower. There was her voice telling him she was coming, followed by a swear as she appeared to hit an appendage on something before the door was opened.

Macleod was taken aback as Hope stood in front of him wrapped in a towel with another around her head.

"Hello, sir. Apologies but running a bit late. I'll be a minute, come in."

Macleod knew he should simply excuse himself and he would see her next door when she was ready. But he could not help but stare at her legs and wrapped up body as she turned round and pulled out a seat for him. He saw the crop top, leggings and hoodie on the bed and for a moment thought she was going to change right in front of him. This would not do.

He remembered his wife changing in his bedroom, one of those conceits of married life. It was always enjoyable seeing her body as she would talk to him about something mundane. Occasionally he would even sneak up on her and give her a cuddle and then...

"Sir?"

"Sorry, McGrath, was somewhere else. I'll go next door, Allinson's waiting. We need an extra cup too."

"Yeah, I know sir. I could do with speaking to you first though," said Hope.

"Well I can hardly stand here, you need to get some clothes on."

"Most men don't complain," teased Hope.

He should have said something simple like *I'm sure they don't* but instead he stayed silent, standing there. He did not look away but was still looking at her as she turned towards him. And then there was a moment of recognition. She should have seemed embarrassed, told him it was best for him to wait outside, which was the sensible thing to do. But she stood and looked at him.

Inside something leapt, a spark of life that had been dead for so long. The memory of his wife being like this with him watching her flooded his mind and then he began to feel ashamed. This was not his wife. This was McGrath, his deputy. She unwrapped the towel covering her hair and the wet mass of red hair fell onto her shoulders and he saw the small cross jangle at the top of her cleavage.

"I'll change in the bathroom," said Hope, smiling. "But we need to keep the voices down as I think these walls are paper thin."

"Okay," said Macleod, "but what's so important?"

Hope disappeared into the bathroom but left the door open. Taking a seat, Macleod looked at the essentials on Hope's desk. She had a few books, one a raunchy novel which made him almost shake his head. On top of it was a commentary on the state of Africa, a book on literature and finally a walking guide. Beside these was a hairbrush, remains of red hair still attached. And then there was a packet of *ladies things* as Macleod always knew them. His wife always kept her sanitary products hidden and Macleod blushed slightly seeing them.

"I wanted to tell you about Allinson. He's not just here for a briefing, although I think that will be useful. We might have some, relations, later. I wanted to check if you were okay with that."

Something in Macleod was not okay with it but it was not the business of policing that was the issue. He recognised the pang of jealousy.

"If it doesn't interfere with the job, it's none of my business. You are free to do as you wish. Just don't flaunt it in public.

Not that I'm suggesting you would." His eyes roamed the room as he felt anger at himself for being attracted to this woman. And then he saw her in the mirror. It was a clear view into the bathroom and she was rubbing herself down, her back to him. He wanted to turn away but found he could not.

"I thought it best I ask," said Hope, "just as we haven't worked together before. I don't do this a lot by the way. Just feeling a bit, well, you know."

"Yes, well, as I said, you don't need to ask, or explain." Looking at her bare behind he realised how much he missed the touch, the feel of his wife. Or was it simply of a woman? She was gone and yet he felt like he was betraying her, here and now.

"There's nothing decided of course, he's just here for a drink tonight. He had asked me to dinner but with what's happening later that was put to bed."

"Of course," said Macleod, "you don't need to explain. As long as you are ready tonight, I don't care." Except I do, he thought. Dear God, what is this? Is this temptation, because it feels like a gift?

Hope turned round and there was the briefest moment when she saw him looking. Her towel had been covering most things but as he spun his head away, he saw her smile.

"You said we need a cup, sir? I have them in the cupboard space below the kettle. Would you grab one?"

"Of course." Something inside burned, a hunger. "And as we are starting to know each other better, Hope, and need to work more closely, you can call me Seoras."

Hope stepped out of the bathroom in her underwear and her crop top. "Seoras, sir?"

"It's Gaelic."

"Seoras. It suits you." She turned back into the bathroom but he knew the image of her standing there smiling as she took in his name was being imprinted onto his brain for keeping.

A few moments later, Hope stepped out and reached past him for her hair brush. Standing in front of the mirror, she took long raking brushes of her red hair and he lapped up the vision. Again, he had not seen a woman do this in so long. Yes, he had missed the physical things with his wife but these simple but intimate acts of grooming were things men did not see that often, unless they shared a room. He watched her arched body as she focused hard on her job.

"I'll go next door, otherwise Allinson will be getting worried."

"Okay, Seoras." Hope smiled and Macleod stopped beside her.

"Only between you and me though. Out there, I'm sir and you're McGrath."

"Of course. You must tell me about this place sometime."

"I doubt it will be of any help in the case, it was twenty years ago."

"I know, Seoras. But it is still bothering you. Something is bothering you being here. It's not that difficult to see."

He nodded and placed a hand on her shoulder. "Yes Hope, but keep that to yourself."

Macleod, with cup in hand, left the bedroom and took the few steps to his own. As he went to swipe with his key card he stopped. His hand was shaking as a memory struck his mind. It had been their honeymoon and they had saved to get away to Portugal. And after all the excitement of the wedding, the mass of family and friends, they had finally gotten to being alone. Having saved themselves for each other, he remembered coming up to their room from outside his hotel.

They had stood watching the sun at the beach and she had told him to wait for twenty minutes before coming up. At the time he was excited but also a bit confused. His father had told him how his mother was forever getting ready but this was not that. Leaving the stunning sun streaking its last furore before sunset, he had climbed the stairs all the way to the eighth floor before standing outside their room. Knocking the door, he had watched it open to the greatest vision he had seen in his life. And once the young man had seen past the delight of her beauty, he had also seen the wonder of her, how she was one of life's restricted souls, held down by systems and suspicions.

Standing at his door now, about to knock, it all flooded back. "I'll just be a moment," he spluttered at the door and walked off. He thought he heard Allinson acknowledge but he did not care. Walking quickly, he rounded the end of the corridor and looked out the window in the wall. The gas works looked back at him but he did not see them. He saw very little. Eyes welling up, he sniffed back pain and hurt, he pushed against the lonely feeling that had haunted him since she had left him.

His father had never cried, never shown any weakness. As he grew up he had been taught to show no emotion but she had shown him emotion, all sorts. Together and alone they had worn themselves on metaphorical sleeves. But as much as he got closer, he eventually saw her pain and did so little about it. In their private world, they were happy but the invasion of this rigid house of cards they lived in broke her and he did so little to fight it. And so he cried.

Jesus wept. That was what she had said to him. Jesus wept. The man, the God he had followed since youth, was brought alive by her in their pain. He had drawn so close with her. But then He let her rip herself away. *Why? Fucking why?*

104

A hand slipped into his and he turned to see Hope's face. "I've given Allinson some nonsense about you having a tick that needs to be got rid of. Take your time, Seoras."

Chapter 16

Macleod dragged himself from his bed and looked in the mirror. After his meeting with Hope and Allinson, he had gone to bed with the desire of getting a few hours' sleep before the night-time trip they had planned. But he had barely slept. His time in Hope's room mixed with memories of the past and all he had done was to go over why his wife had left this world, and why he was finding himself deeply attracted to the younger Detective on his team.

Flicking on the bathroom light, he heard the fan begin to drone and he switched on the shower. Stepping into the bath and then pulling the curtain across, he felt the blast of the shower, like it was trying to sweep him away. But the water felt good on his tense shoulders and he stood still as it did its work.

By the time he had dressed, he thought he heard movement from next door. Hope and Allinson had retired from his room and headed towards the bar and he had mixed feelings about this rendezvous. He was putting his feelings for Hope down to the trauma of coming back to the island and reliving his wife's death. Hope was providing a boon and after such a long time with no intimacy, it was no wonder he was falling for a woman who was reaching out to his pain. But he knew it was not the real thing. It could not be.

Putting on a short jacket, he exited his room and stood in front of Hope's. Knocking gently, he stood and waited as he heard her moving about. The door opened presently and the red head was standing before him in her boots and jeans with a floppy cream sweater on.

"Come in, I'm just about ready," said Hope looking a little bleary eyed.

Macleod stepped in as Hope retired to the bathroom, presumably to fix her hair which was still looking much wilder than he could remember. As he stood at her table, he looked at the bed and noted it had only been slept in by one. He felt a tinge of delight at this and then chastised himself for his foolish feelings. *Dear God, what a mess I am.*

Returning from the bathroom, Hope was tying her hair up in a ponytail and looked with concern at Macleod. He nodded back what he trusted was a convincing stance of being alright but he was not sure it had worked. She was a detective, after all, and like himself could read people. They made their way downstairs to the car and Macleod let Hope drive to the Castle grounds where they parked in the almost empty car park at Lews castle.

"So, where to from here," asked Hope, stepping out of the car.

"We take the path up into the grounds. The place she indicated is a small pool with a garden close to the river. It makes sense as she could watch us arrive without being seen. She said alone but I don't go to see potential murderers on my own at night."

Together the pair started their walk and Macleod found himself remembering childhood days spent around the paths of the grounds, hiding out here and there. But he also remembered a young woman taking him on midnight walks by the river in the grounds and his first kiss. Although they had waited until marriage to become fully intimate, they had *made out* as the kids today said, many times by the river.

He tried to focus on the job in hand but the quiet as they walked was leading him into deeper thoughts and so he decided to break the silence.

"How did your evening go?" asked Macleod.

"Well there really wasn't much evening left. We had a quick drink and then I hit my bed. I think he was disappointed."

"You're in the middle of a case and about to get up a few hours later. I think he was lucky to get a drink with you."

"I think he was wanting more, Seoras. I thought I was wanting more too but I just felt tired in the end. It's not like me."

"We were always told that there was nothing wrong with waiting. I waited with my wife for years until we were married and I don't regret it. Not that anyway. You have to understand that growing up here, you at least said all the right things. We used to walk these paths and if you look over there beside that path, that was a favourite spot for us. You can see the sun come up, although we saw little sun. Saw plenty of each other."

"Sounds like you were quite the guy back then," said Hope with a grin.

"She was quite a woman. Not a tart, not putting it on offer for whoever. But when she had settled on me, we had our moments. In those days we didn't have the same sort of understanding about it all that your education gives you these days. I think we had more fun finding out. These days I guess it's expected to go much further, earlier."

"I hope I'm a bit stronger than that, Seoras. I enjoy the physical as much as anyone, maybe more but it's on my terms. Ask Allinson."

There was just a hint of explanation about what had happened earlier in the evening and Macleod thought it best not to push it. But again that delight at Hope not having been engaged with another man flared. *I'm such a daft fool.*

Macleod remembered summer on the island always producing long hours of daylight and tonight had been no exception. But now at two in the morning the darkness had finally arrived and he actually felt cool. Not cold but cool, as if something was wrong and he should feel warmer. Maybe it was his age or maybe just that his body should not be awake at this hour. He wondered if Hope felt the same. If so, she did not show it.

The paths in the Lews Castle grounds snaked here and there but there was no sign of any person. The sounds of a sleeping port were there in the background but the occasional scurry could be heard, a nocturnal creature on the move. He remembered kids bringing alcohol up here when he was younger but maybe the hour was too late for that. It was also the Sabbath and in his day getting caught like that on a Sunday morning was not to be contemplated.

As they came over a rise in the path, Macleod saw the compact garden with the pond. There was a bench at one side and sitting there was a young woman. She was small, wrapped up in a hoodie which covered her hair but she had the curves of a woman. Macleod thought he saw her shoulders tense as she saw him and he stopped Hope and turned to his partner.

"Maybe you should wait outside the garden, she is only expecting one person."

"Are you sure, Seoras, she did clock you last time?" said Hope.

"I do remember, but she is obviously scared I don't want her to run. She's already tense from what I'm seeing."

"Okay, but I'll keep you in view."

Macleod went on alone and watched the young woman as he approached. She was holding a can in one hand, probably a cider or beer, but it was too dark for Macleod's eyes to see. He walked along the triangular perimeter until he found the gate to the garden. The neat path inside was markedly different to the large paths of the grounds and Macleod appreciated the effort put in to maintain this spot. Turning on the path, he stood beside the bench the woman was sitting on. He thought that she had played this wrong. With Hope on the outside and himself beside her, the woman would have difficulty making an escape. Of course maybe she didn't want to.

"You wanted to see me?" asked Macleod.

"I believe you wanted me," said the girl in a sarcastic tone.

"Yes. I'm investigating Sara's death, and you are one of her closest friends. Am I right in that respect?"

"Friend. Do you think I ran away because I was her friend? He found out about us, he realised that she wasn't what he had hoped for. Bloody bastard."

"Do you mind if I sit down?" asked Macleod, sitting before he received an answer. "Who found out?"

"This man. This client. I told her not to do it but she never listened to anyone, Sara. The whole massage parlour business. I said it was whorish what she was doing but then Sara never saw anything wrong in using her body to get what she wanted."

"Did that bother you?"

"Of course it bloody did. Do you know how shit it feels to

hear your lover groaning away on another? And a man at that when you know she prefers women. Not that she would ever let that be known."

"This man, was he the one on the photo on your wall. The three of you were there in it."

The woman nodded. "You found that. I was hoping you might be a half decent cop. Bet you're finding this place a bit dire after Glasgow or wherever you came up from."

Dire, thought Macleod, *you have no idea.* "Why did you hit me then?"

"I thought you might be him. I couldn't see you properly and hit you before I knew it was you. And then, well, I'd hit a copper."

"But I shouted Police when I entered," reasoned Macleod.

"And that means what? Absolute shit all. Still could have been anyone."

"Did you see him kill her?"

"No. But I left them there. Out near the pier you are all getting excited over. Where all your teams and that are. It's weird, copper, that pier is like sacred in a way. We did it right there. Many times. Out of the way and it became our place. And then he took that away when he took her too." She broke down crying, sniffing hard and eventually spitting out the mess of snot that had built up in her mouth. There was nothing elegant in this mourning, nothing delicate. The girl turned and fell into Macleod's arms and he almost panicked until he realised she was breaking down.

"Let it out," said Macleod.

"She was mine. Do you understand? They didn't own her, she was mine and every damn one of them wanted a piece of her. If it hadn't have been for her mum, she would never have had bothered with any of them. She was mine!"

The voice echoed around the small garden surrounded as it was on all sides. But beyond the sobs of this poor woman, Macleod heard something else.

"I left him with her, I shouldn't have left her. I shouldn't have..."

Macleod heard a cry from Hope. Standing up and turning, he saw a large man dressed in black with a balaclava coming towards him. Further up the path, he saw another man approaching as well as one beyond that, right where Hope had been.

He reached down and grabbed the woman's shoulder. "Get up and go. You need to go." The girl was still sobbing and Macleod realised the man was close. A large stick was raised by the man and Macleod side-stepped as he brought it down. Throwing a punch into the man's side, he found himself being pushed aside and the man was now closest to the woman. She cowered as she realised her situation and Macleod saw the beating about to unfold. He ran the few paces the man now had on him and threw himself at him. Together they tumbled into the small pond.

Chapter 17

Macleod rolled in the shallow water, fighting for purchase on the man. The brute was strong and Macleod took a knee in the side. Breaking the surface, he gasped before being hit on the shoulder. This broke the man free and Macleod fought the pain to scramble to his feet.

The girl was running down the path, following the path down the river. Two men were in pursuit, followed by Hope. Macleod ran out of the small garden and followed, his feet splodging as he made his way beside the water. The river fell into small pools of calm before tumbling down rocks but the path descended slowly, its gravelly surface occasionally failing to give purchase.

Macleod saw the girl scrambling out onto rocks, trying to cross the river. He was close now but Hope was closer and had caught up on one of the men in black. She grabbed him by the shoulder and Macleod saw him turn and catch Hope with an uppercut to the jaw. She rocked momentarily before grabbing the man and taking him to the ground.

Macleod arrived and thought about assisting but the other man in black was jumping across rocks out into the middle of the water, right behind the girl. Jumping onto a grass covered rock Macleod nearly fell but recovered to throw himself onto the next one. He was definitely getting too old for this but the spirit drove him on. And then he saw the knife brandished by the man. He had the girl by the shoulder and the knife was raised.

Flinging himself from the rock he stood on, Macleod leapt, stretching as far as possible and managed to get a hand on the man's arm, causing him to tumble with Macleod into the river. The force of the river took hold and swept the two men over a small drop into an idle pool. Before he could react, Macleod felt two hands drive his head down into the water and his breath blew out in panic.

He placed two hands above him, finding the attackers hands but with no platform, he could not drive them off his head. He felt his strength waning and the panic beginning to fill his body. His hands now sought purchase on anything and he grabbed something in the dark of the water. It was a leg. He placed a second hand on the leg and understood the orientation of it. Without hesitation, he moved his hands up the leg and found the man's genitals. Then he squeezed as hard as he could, his life depending on it.

The hands lifted from his head and he raced to the surface, desperate to grab some air. Gulping down the cool night, he saw his attacker climbing back out onto the side of the river. The knife was gone from his hands but he was moving back towards the girl's location. She was now nearly across the body of water but the man seemed desperate as he reached the rocks that would carry him across again.

Hope arrived without any other attacker in sight and Macleod watched her pursue the man onto the rocks as he made again for the girl. Reaching down, Hope grabbed his leg, causing him to fall. The man kicked out hard hitting Hope in the head. He heard her cry out and watched the man turn. He pummelled two hard blows to her head but she managed to keep fighting as the man stood over her, and swept his legs from under him by scissoring his legs with her own.

Macleod was back on the edge of the river and climbed out, desperate to aid his colleague. The man had gotten to his feet again and was holding Hope by the neck. She looked woozy, as if she was about to collapse. Seeing Macleod, the man looked for the girl but she had disappeared on the far shore. The man swore to the night and continued to throttle Hope. Macleod ran hard towards the rocks and saw he could cut the man off.

"It's over," blurted Macleod, his breath still struggling to catch up with his actions. "You have to get past me and your friends have gone. And the one you wanted is gone too. So stand down. It's over."

"Like hell. I have your bitch, copper. She's not doing so well." *He's not joking*, thought Macleod, *she looks about to drop*.

The man held Hope at a distance and punched her twice to the head with a force that scared Macleod. "I guess I'm leaving, copper, you'd better get her." With that, the man dropped Hope into the river. Macleod watched her fall, noting there was no scream, no effort to save herself. The detective in him wanted to go for the man but with the girl now clear of the scene, he had to save Hope. Macleod jumped into the water and swam after Hope's floating body.

Her body went over the small drop Macleod had fallen down previously and he followed. Once into the pool, he kicked hard, fighting to maintain the surface but reached out a hand and grabbed her leg. Her floppy sweater provided further purchase and soon he had her head. The river had diluted the blood on her face making a watery red cover but Macleod saw that wounds were still open. Supporting her neck, he kicked hard to the side of the river.

As he pulled himself onto the rocks, he heard her moan. "Thank you, God," he said out loud, and dragged her out of the pond onto the side. Looking around he saw no one. The river cascaded on and the gush of running water was constant but otherwise he heard nothing.

Macleod took out his mobile but it did not work. He searched Hope for her own but again it did nothing, the water obviously affecting them.

At six foot, Hope was actually slightly taller than Macleod, although more shapely. He thought she would be better at carrying him. He placed her before him and kneeled down taking her onto his shoulder. *You shouldn't say this about a woman* he thought, *but she's damn heavy. Come on girl, hang on.*

Macleod stumbled along knowing he had a long walk back to anywhere that was not off the beaten track. He continued down by the river, mainly because going downhill was easier at this time. And then over the river he heard something. There was a giggle, definitely a giggle. Then a sloppy sound, like a kiss, but a prolonged one, not a quick peck. He saw a foot sticking out from behind a rock.

"Whoever's in there, we need your help," shouted Macleod.

A young man jumped up, maybe eighteen and was pulling his belt tight around his jeans. Behind him a girl emerged, dressing quickly.

"What the hell? You bloody perv, you…" The man's tirade stopped as he evidently caught sight of Hope's bloodied face. "Oh God, Jesus, look at her. Man, what the…"

"Have you a phone, son? A mobile, tell me you have a damn

mobile."

"Yes," said the man pulling one from his pocket.

"Nine, nine, nine, now! Ambulance now! Ring the damn thing."

Macleod collapsed onto the ground and gently laid Hope down. As he rolled over and laid on his back, he felt a hand grab his and a faint voice speak to him.

"Shit Seoras, that bastard. Did she get away? Did she go?"

"Yeah, she's gone. They are too but not in her direction."

Hope tapped his hand and lay silent again. Macleod heard the young man on the telephone being questioned by the operator, giving out directions. He told the man he was Police and to relay that. And then he lay on his back, feeling the pain of where he had been hit. Rolling over again he looked at Hope, her eyes closed.

"You still there? Talk to me Hope, talk to me."

"Yeah, still here. Wish I wasn't but still bloody here. If I see that bastard again, I'll castrate him. I must look like shit." Hope didn't open her eyes the whole time she spoke and Macleod could not help but worry.

"Look at me Hope, open those eyes and look at me." Macleod watched her turn her head and stare at him. "I'm sorry, I should have protected you. It's not right a man hitting a woman. I've never had a female officer attacked with me before. I'm sorry."

"Shut up you dinosaur. I did more damage than you did." Hope laughed and then choked a little. "God, that hurt."

"Hey mister," said the young man, "that's the ambulance and shit coming. Can I go? We shouldn't be here. If her Dad finds out she's been here…"

Macleod laughed out loud despite the pain he felt. "What's your name, son?"

117

"Donald, sir."

"Okay Donald, did you see anything else before we arrived here?"

"Eh, no. We were kinda, busy, you know."

"Second name, Donald, what's your second name?"

"Macleod."

Seoras laughed again, of course it was. "Did the operator get your details, address and that?"

"Yes, oh hell, yes they did. They'll come and interview us, man that'll put us in the shit."

"Stay until the ambulance or someone gets here Donald, I'll tell them to keep it quiet. You have been a great help."

Donald seemed relieved. "Thanks, man."

"No Donald, thank you, and Donald, next time, get somewhere a bit more salubrious for her. I mean it's a bit rough and ready out here."

Macleod realised he was giving advice on mating to this man when he should have been outraged that they had been out here at all. *Still*, he thought, *without them we wouldn't be getting any help and it's a blooming long walk back. God, you provide the weirdest support sometimes.*

The first responder to arrive was a policeman on foot, shortly followed by paramedics. Macleod waved away attention and pointed to Hope, who although quiet was still conscious. It was not long before she was being carried away on a stretcher by the local Coastguard rescue team, back to where the ambulance had been abandoned. Macleod was able to walk back, sore but generally in a reasonable condition. He had requested a search for the girl who he thought was still in great danger. As he reached the temporary shelter that had been erected at Cuddy Point the small slipway across from the town centre, he asked for the Police search co-ordinator.

A man in a blue jumpsuit approached and he recognised him as one of the Coastguards.

"Where's our man? I was looking for the POLSAR." asked Macleod.

"Been handed to me as we don't have a POLSAR here yet. I have teams from the Coastguard, Police and Mountain Rescue looking for her. We'll try for the helicopter as well. Won't be easy if she's trying to hide."

"Okay. I'll get out of your way."

"Thank you. And if you don't mind me saying you should go and get checked out, they said you went under the water."

"Okay, I hear you. I'm going to see my colleague anyway, but thanks again."

And Macleod felt like a spare end. Allinson had seemed to get everything going in a place where he was struggling to work out how everything ran. Back in Glasgow, things would have been different but up here, Macleod guessed they had to use whatever resources were available.

A car took Macleod to the hospital and he was taken in to Accident and Emergency to get checked over. Once the doctor was happy he was not at risk, Macleod made his way into the hospital and asked for Hope's room. She had been transferred up from A&E for the night to get some rest and to be monitored.

On arrival at the ward, Macleod was taken to a private room. The light was on inside and he knocked the door. On a positive answer, he stepped inside and saw Hope sat up in bed with a medical gown over her. The long ponytail of red hair was now gone and her feisty crown was now splayed over her shoulders. Macleod thought it suited her.

119

"Hey, you okay?" asked Hope.

"No slower than normal. You?"

"Feel like shit. My jaws been pummelled, my head hurts and my body's crying out but otherwise fine. It's all just bruising thankfully. I wouldn't have been surprised if I'd broken something."

"You took a pounding. Sorry, I should have stopped him. It's not right."

"I'm a police woman, Seoras, this is part of the job."

Macleod shook his head. "It's not right for a woman to be in the line of fire like that. Sorry, I know what you'll say and what the boss will say but it ain't right."

"Cut that now, or I'll get angry. It's a different world and I signed up for this, so shut it, sir," said Hope standing up. "Is their canteen open? I'm starving. You can buy me breakfast."

"I'll wait outside," said Macleod.

"Don't be daft," said Hope, turning around looking inside the small cupboards beside her bed. The medical gown with its opening at the back revealed a view of Hope's bottom. He knew he should turn away but Macleod stared. *She just looks so good.*

"There's it." With her back to him, Hope untied the medical gown, before wrapping herself in her dressing gown. Again Macleod told himself to look away but again failed. Only his wife had ever changed so brazenly in front of him. He remembered it well.

Hope turned around and approached Macleod and placed a hand on each shoulder. She leaned forward and gently kissed his forehead. "Thank you. That was a lot closer than I ever imagined it would be."

Macleod saw her start to weep, her eyes becoming flooded

and then she grabbed him, holding him tight. He held her and wrapped arms around her. He raised his hand and ran it through her hair in what he thought was a comforting manner. He gently kissed her forehead before tilting her head back to look at her. Her eyes, watering with tears looked back.

He felt an urge to wrap this woman up in his arms and sweep her onto the bed. To love away all the pain she was feeling. She was so under his skin. But was she, or was it just the memories of his wife and their similarities at times that was causing this passionate revival? He didn't know and just stared. Then Hope buried her head in his chest and cried.

Later, as he waited for Hope to put on some trousers, he realised one of the things that had stopped any further union of them had been the height issue. Hope was an inch taller than he and when he had tried to hold her to his chest, it just felt awkward. His wife had been three inches smaller and perfect to hold to.

When Hope tapped his shoulder, he had convinced himself, all these feelings were just the maelstrom the memories of his wife had brought up. As he watched her exit the room, doubts began to fester on the premise formed.

Chapter 18

Macleod left Hope in the hospital. The medical staff had said they wanted to observe her for at least twelve more hours and Macleod knew she needed rest. The poor woman had taken a pummelling at the man's hands and was fortunate not to have any broken bones or serious injury beyond bruising. When he had left her, her jaw had started to swell and a dark bruise was forming.

And yet he felt like he had lost a limb. After popping by the station, where he picked up a temporary mobile phone, Macleod headed to the mobile command point that was co-ordinating the search for the young woman. She was in trouble, given how the thugs had gone after her but where she was, was a mystery. By this time, Macleod reckoned she would be far away from the castle grounds but you never knew with people, especially those on the run. If they were merely lost then you could reasonably predict their movements to some degree, but those on the run could always play a wild card.

On arrival at the command point he was surprised to see the council woman in attendance, talking to Allinson. Macleod's suspicious mind kicked in and he waited politely for the councillor to finish with his junior before catching his eye.

"What does she want?" he asked the Detective once the

woman had moved away.

"Was giving the old anything-the-council-can-do-to-help speech, sir. Wasting my time really. She was trying to get details about where we were looking, surreptitiously mind, but get them all the same."

Macleod grimaced. "Do we know where she was last night?"

"No, sir. But you said all the thugs were men."

"And they were. Doesn't mean someone else wasn't watching. I'll have a word with her. I take it there's no update."

"No, sir. We've had them searching all night but by now the area she could be in is massive. We're continuing with the helicopter and search teams at the moment but if she's not found by this afternoon, we're back into having an area the size of the island really."

"Have you checked the ferries?"

"Yes sir, and we have got people to the ports and slipways, advised the harbours, but it's not simple. We haven't got the manpower to cover something that wide. The other emergency services are helping but we can't involve the public." Allinson hung his head, looking somewhat dejected. "How's Hope, sir?"

"Detective McGrath is somewhat battered and the hospital is going to hold onto her a wee while longer. But she's good, Allinson, she's okay. She saved the woman last night."

"So did you, I hear, sir."

"It was McGrath that saved the day, Allinson. Quite a detective." Macleod meant this as a genuine compliment to her ability to do her job but he saw Allinson's smile and knew he was somewhere else with his thoughts.

"Heck of a woman, sir. Hard to read though. Thought I was in there to be honest, and then blown straight out."

123

"Probably just dedicated to the case, Allinson, as we all should be. I've been told to rest as well, so after I've spoken to the councillor I shall pop along to church. I have my mobile if anything turns up." Allinson nodded and Macleod turned away and spotted the council woman walking away from the Cuddy Point mobile base along the road that would eventually lead back to the golf club, where any cars generally parked on a Sunday.

Macleod thought how in his days on the island, there would be no cars near this area as the gates would be closed. But he had been told that the Lews castle would be open for guests and those wanting a coffee on a Sunday as well as a few other places in town. *Things do change*, he thought, *but slowly*.

"Councillor Smith," he shouted after speeding up to close the gap between them.

The woman turned round. "Ah, Detective, do call me, Marie. How is your colleague? I hear she took quite a beating last night. At least that's what the ambulance driver said."

"Yes, but she's fine, Mrs Smith, just a bit battered." Walking alongside the woman, Macleod realised that no one was asking how he was, and the bruises seemed to smart all the more because of it. "Sorry to be abrupt, but can I ask your location last night. As someone with a key link to Sara Hewitt, you can understand why I need to ask you this."

"But of course, Detective," said Marie Smith, but Macleod could tell she had hoped he wouldn't ask it. "I was in bed, like all good people should be."

"Forgive me but this case has been an eye opener," said Macleod. "Was anyone with you?"

"Yes they were, Detective, but it is sensitive. You see, he has a wife."

"That wouldn't go down well with the public here, Mrs Smith. I take it he has a name?" Macleod looked straight at the woman, making sure she knew he was going to have this name.

"Have you breakfasted, Detective? What say we take a walk up to the castle and find a quiet corner to discuss this matter?"

"Okay, but we will discuss it. And you may have to make a statement to the effect of what you tell me."

The woman waved a hand. "Of course, Detective, of course, happy to help, now let's get a move on, I am hungry."

Macleod did not like to say but he was hungry too despite having breakfasted with Hope. As he walked the short distance to the castle, Macleod noted the various paths that swung amongst the trees of the grounds. They seemed newly gravelled and there was a general air of industry about the place despite it being a Sunday.

"The Sabbath has changed here somewhat," said the Councillor on noting Macleod looking around. "Plenty of dog walkers and that but they still shut off what they can. I tell them we need to open up the place, encourage our tourists. But you have to be careful how quick you push progress, many of the people here still follow what is said on a Sunday. And a lot of those pulpits preach a day of nothing."

"A day of quiet and reflection on our Lord actually, Mrs Smith. I believe they see it as following a biblical principal."

"Actually, I think some just like a quiet day. But it goes too far. Too restrictive. Things need to change, to be more open."

Macleod wondered how open the council woman's electorate would be as to her paying for sex with another woman. This was not Glasgow. But his mind also drifted back to Sundays with his wife. Sure they had gone to church twice a day, out in the country community they had belonged to, but they had not stayed inside during the day if they could. No, she always wanted him to go out, to take her places. They had been careful, gone away from prying eyes.

The day they took a picnic out to the moor and had sat down by the loch. Everything was still and she was in her summer dress on a day of sun, something the island was not famous for. It had been a tick that had started it, the wee blighters that could crawl up your leg and one had seen fit to make it up his wife's leg, right to the inside of her thigh.

After removing the offending creature, he had been leaning over her in a rather compromising position. He had been looking around hoping no one would see this crude setup on a Sunday but then she had excited him in those private ways and things had developed. The swim in the loch and subsequent act of passion was still clear to him. If they had been caught it would have been a scandal, yet it was one of his favourite memories of her. Everyone talked about missing her as a wife but he had lost his lover. While not being the only thing he missed about her, it was one that had not been replaced to any degree. No wonder he burned at times, as the good book says.

"Have you been in our castle?"

The voice brought Macleod back to reality and he shook his head. "Not yet. Please lead the way."

The Councillor led Macleod along an ornate hallway before taking a right turn through a door into a covered but light cafe. The ceiling above him was glass and he quickly recognised he was in an old courtyard space that had been changed into a roomy cafe. The modern tables were set out at a generous distance and the councillor took his order while he sat down. His hips ached as he sat and he could feel some of his bruises smarting. *Hope must be feeling a lot worse*, he thought.

Placing a small wooden spoon in a vase on the table, the councillor sat down and brushed down her skirt. Apparently something had fallen on it but Macleod could not work out what. The drinks arrived quickly and Macleod sought the sugar from a carousel at the wall before returning to his coffee. As he sipped the hot liquid, Marie Smith looked at him, taking great pains to show her turmoil.

"I'm not normally into affairs, Inspector, but I think we were really caught off guard by each other. His marriage is practically dead anyway, I think she's not, as they say, active for him. And well, I have been missing the physical."

Macleod noticed she was leaning forward and he felt a foot touch his leg. The councillor removed her jacket hanging it behind her seat and when she turned back, she leaned towards Macleod, her blouse hanging low. He actually felt sick with this brazen display.

"That's not what I had heard, Councillor, indeed I was under the impression you paid for sex with females."

The woman's face fell. Obviously she knew Macleod would have known about Sara, but maybe she was more angry that her charms were not working on him. But she moved back into her seat and continued.

"Well, I do have needs, Inspector, and if you can satisfy them from two angles why not. But trust me, I do need a man's touch. And the air of danger with this affair I think went straight to my head."

Macleod shook his head. "I don't care about your reasons. What you do with another woman's husband is up to you and them, not me, unless you breech the law. What does matter is I have a young woman scared and on the run and I need to close off potential lines of enquiry. So, who is he? Where can I get in touch with him? And quickly."

"You could take a leaf from your Detective McGrath. Lot more subtle. In all respects, I think. His name is Alastair McKinney. You'll find him at church this morning, the United Free Reformed Presbyterian up from the station. It's not a church, they just use a hall as they are a breakaway faction from one of the other ones."

"Which one?" asked Macleod.

"God knows."

"I'm sure he does, Mrs Smith. So you were with him last night? From when until when?"

"Well, we met at ten o'clock out at the car park towards Arnish, opposite the back end of the grounds. We left my car and took his out towards Lochs where we turned off to a small caravan he has, near the peats he cuts. I left there about five this morning with him and took a message from one of my constituents who works in the hospital. They told me about the palaver you had last night and so I popped down this morning to see if I could assist."

There was no sweat on the woman, no sign of nerves. This bothered Macleod. A councillor potentially getting caught with another wife's husband and she's not flinching. Unless…, maybe there are worse things.

"I'll check with him directly this morning. After all, I think we all owe the Lord a look in on His day. Whatever else you do with your day, Mrs Smith, and I'm sure you need some rest after an…, shall we say, energetic night, spend some time with your maker."

"Most thoughtful of you, Inspector. Most thoughtful."

"Thank you for the coffee. Big difference from the last

time I set eyes on here," said Macleod leaving with a wave of acknowledgement.

He had been totally determined to keep his past from anyone but he needed to test the water with Mrs Smith. *Let's see how much she wants to get involved,* thought Macleod. *I bet she won't wait until the Sabbath is over.*

Chapter 19

The walk from Lews castle through the grounds to the small bridge that crossed the river as it let out to the sea, was refreshing. Macleod felt he was finally playing some cards in this whole game and he was keen to see the results. The air felt good and he even thought that the bruises had somehow gone down somewhat on his body. Positive mental attitude, that's what his boss would say.

The town had become alive but only in the sense that a patient in a coma is more alive than someone deceased. Smartly dressed men in dark suits and women in hats drove by in cars on their way to church. A few walked and gave him a nod as they passed. He was in his usual shirt and tie as befitted an inspector but he still felt a little underdressed.

At church in Glasgow, very few women wore hats, and it was by choice rather than precedent. In fact Macleod had seen men arrive in less than a tie as well. The island certainly held to the traditions a lot stronger than the mainland. He heard solitary bells ringing across various steeples and fell in line behind others now having exited their cars and continuing on foot.

At the door of the hall that served as a church, Macleod was greeted by a stout man in a black suit. A handshake that could have taken your arm off ensued and Macleod winced as the muscles in his body reminded him they had done enough last night and did not need any heavy handed welcomes.

"Good morning, a fine Sabbath day."

"Indeed," said Macleod, remembering to just smile. Entering the hall, he took a seat at the back and watched as the church filled up to almost half full. He was in good company in his choice of seat as apart from some men who were sitting together at the front, presumably the elders, everyone sat at the rear half.

The minister appeared after everyone had sat in silence for some five minutes and the service opened with a psalm sung by a presenter while the congregation accompanied him. No one stood as that was reserved for the prayer that ensued when the singing stopped. One of the men from the front prayed for a solid ten minutes and again Macleod's body told him off. These activities were not unusual to Macleod, for his own church in Glasgow was similar but somewhat jollier.

The service lasted an hour and a half and the sermon left Macleod in no doubt that an unrepentant sinner would be going to hell. *The Gospel preached*, thought Macleod, *and my wife was no sinner, she was a believer. Yet the number who told me she was going to hell after the incident. The same people who criticised her when she tried to be different, when she was struggling.*

With the service ended, Macleod strode over to one of the elders, reaching forward with a handshake so the man had to respond. Leaning forward he whispered in his ear the name "Alastair McKinney" and the man nodded with his head to a man with his back to them. Thanking the elder, Macleod made his way to McKinney and tapped him on the shoulder.

"May I have a word?" asked Macleod.

"Oh, hello. You're a policeman aren't you? I guess I should always have a word with you when requested." The man was tripping over his own laugh, it was so forced. There was a nervousness to his shoulders as well.

"Shall your wife accompany us? I wouldn't want her to worry where you had gone."

"No," said the man, sweeping a hand across his jet black, greasy hair. "She'll be fine here, she knows to wait."

"Really, almost prophetic in her approach considering she doesn't know what I want. You might not come back." Macleod sneered and saw the man start to panic.

"I'll just say to her," the man said quickly, "and Macleod watched him speak to a woman some ten years or so younger than the man. She nodded and then smiled at Macleod. "This way," indicated the man leading Macleod to a side room.

On entering a room that held a table and some chairs with some of the most hideous wallpaper Macleod had ever seen, the man spun around and stood with his head hung low. His hands were shaking.

"I have been told by Councillor Smith, that you entered into sexual relations with her last night. Is that correct?"

"Yes," McKinney said quickly. "We were together all the time."

"What time?"

"Oh, from ten o'clock."

"Ten o'clock precisely?" snapped Macleod.

"Yes."

"How do you know?"

"Eh… The radio in the car. It gave out the time."

"What station?"

"Eh… Isles FM, the local station, you might not be familiar

132

with it."

"Where did you meet?"

"The car park at the back of the castle grounds. Then we took my car to my caravan. We left at five."

"How did you know it was five?"

"The radio."

I'll need to check that, thought Macleod, *but he's lying. Totally lying.* "How long have you been having sexual relations with Mrs Smith?"

The man looked at Macleod. "Eh, three months."

"And how did you meet? I mean how did you get together the first time?"

Again the man paused, looking to the air for an answer. "I went to her with an issue I was having with our bin collection."

"What issue?"

"They were refusing to collect my bins because they said I was putting commercial waste in them but it's a garage industry so strictly it's actually household waste, do you see? I couldn't believe it when I came home that day and the bin is just sitting there. Anyway it went on for two months until I went to see Mrs Smith and she sorted it. She leaned rather heavily on certain people in the council."

"And for that you gave her sex?" asked Macleod showing a disingenuous face.

"No! Yes! Well, the sex just kind of happened."

The man was one minute riding a rollercoaster with his hands in the air and the next was unable to find the exit, thought Macleod. "How did you do it? With Marie, I mean. What was your favourite position? Two months, I'm sure you had a bit of routine with it to keep each other happy?"

The man was shaking again. "I hardly think we should be

speaking of this in a house of God."

And you certainly should not be lying in here either. "Having been playing away from home, I don't think you should be preaching at me. Now Marie said she liked on top, a lot."

"Right. Err… yes, that's right. On top."

"You've been most helpful, McKinney. Now I think I shall retire and let you get back to your wife."

Macleod opened the door for the man and let him exit first, before following back into the main hall. He watched the man go to his wife and embrace her before glancing back at Macleod with almost pleading eyes. *He's never played away in his life. Look at him. Marie Smith has no real alibi but let's let her think she does.*

There was a small commotion at the far end of the hall and he could hear a few men and women tutting about something. Then there were voices raised, in indignation more than anger but raised all the same. And then through the small gathering he saw the problem. A red haired woman with a pony tail stood in her jeans, and crop top with a blouse lying open. She cut a figure not seen that morning during the service.

Macleod laughed inside and also felt buoyed that his colleague was well enough to be out of hospital. She had a dark bruise on her chin and other marks around her eyes. She also looked exhausted. But amidst the cavalcade of disgust at her attire, she was standing proudly.

"Can we kindly let Detective McGrath through, please? This way, McGrath," shouted Macleod over the small hubbub. He watched Hope make her way over. Taller than most of the women and quite a few of the men, he saw disgust, jealousy and even a few glances of appreciation. His face remained serious but inside he felt a joy that she was back with him.

"What are you doing out and about? You need rest," said Macleod, with a chastening tone.

"No rest for the wicked, sir, isn't that what they say in these buildings," retorted McGrath.

"Well now you are here, you can make yourself useful. Here, take this photo of the mysterious man on the wall and see if anyone here knows him. Quite a few of the congregation will already be outside. And next time, you might consider something a bit more, mundane, for church."

"Something wrong with what I'm wearing?"

There's everything right with that outfit, thought Macleod. *It shows your figure but doesn't make you look like a tart. But it's something else for in here.* "Frankly, to a church crowd like this, you're probably looking like a Jezebel."

"Well then, she must have looked damn fine!" With that Hope took a photo from Macleod and made her way back to the front door and began asking if anyone had seen the man in the photograph. Macleod was briefly accosted by an older lady who tacitly gave comment on Hope's outfit but he was not listening close enough to catch the detail. Instead, Macleod was watching some of the reactions Hope was getting from her questions.

There seemed to be an air of avoidance, a gradual drift away from Hope, almost a bypassing. It was not so blatant as to be obvious but if you watched for a time, you could see how certain people were avoiding the question, or shaking their heads before looking. One elder, a man probably in his fifties and who Macleod had seen sitting at the front of the church, was a prime example of this. Giving Hope a wide berth, he also looked away from her when it would have been normal to take a glance, especially at a woman who looked like Hope.

Macleod put a hand in the air and caught the attention of his red headed colleague. With a point of a finger, he singled out the elder and nodded when Hope mouthed "apprehend". Her blaze of hair stood out above the other heads and Macleod watched her move swiftly and deliberately into the man's path. But he turned away and seemed to be interested in a collection of psalm books on a table.

As Macleod made his way to them, he saw Hope ask the same question she had been asking other people but the man did not even look at the photograph before shaking his head in the negative. Approaching the man from behind, Macleod surprised him.

"If you want we can take you down to the station and make you look at the photograph." The man turned towards Macleod and then desperately scanned around him. A hand was placed on Macleod's shoulder and a voice he recognised from the sermon spoke out in firm but threatening tones.

"I doubt we want to be doing anything rash on the Lord's Day, Detective, probably best we all wait until tomorrow."

The hand on the shoulder was what did it. He remembered such a hand when he had been spoken to about his wife, and her behaviour on a Sabbath Day. It had been hot, a rare occasion and she had been seen on the beach, in a skirt above the knees. It was a skirt he had loved, one that suited her but one that became the subject of nasty finger pointing. He did not take kindly to hands on his shoulder.

"Why exactly, Reverend?"

The man who had laid his hand on him was a couple of inches bigger than Macleod but was also broader and well built. He stepped between Macleod and the shy man and Macleod saw Hope raise her eyebrows.

"This is the Lord's day, Detective, as I know you are aware and I think it best that the day focus on Him and not turn into a charade, a day when the misfortunes of a girl of questionable morals takes centre stage over our Lord's sacrifice. I'm sure if you come back tomorrow..."

"You will move aside or I will have McGrath here, book you for obstruction. The girl of questionable morals is dead, murdered. And at the moment, I have serious suspicion that someone in this building is hiding something from us." Macleod glared at the minister but the man just smiled back.

"They said you were weak in bringing your wife into line, letting her dress as brazenly as your colleague here, and look what became of that. Leave it alone today and enjoy your Sabbath, Detective. I think that would be wise."

If there would have been no repercussions, Macleod would have killed the man. He saw himself burying punch after punch into the man's face, breaking his sanctimonious jaw. *How dare he talk about her! How dare he!*

"McGrath, kindly escort our silent friend outside the building and have him wait there for me. I need a few words with this man of G..., well, this man."

Macleod was not looking at the minister but he could see from Hope's corner of the mouth smile that his words had had the desired effect. As Hope exited with the silent elder, Macleod rounded on the minister.

"There is something unholy in here and you cover up the stink at your peril. Call yourself a man of God and then attack a widower still in his grief. And worse still, cover for a murderer. As the good book says, you brood of vipers. Next time you get in my way, I'll throw everything in the book at you. And it's Detective Inspector."

Macleod walked off without another glance at the minister and met Hope outside where the man was standing with many of the congregation watching from a distance. Macleod pulled out a copy of the photograph and thrust it in the man's face. "Here, or down the station, you decide. But who is this?"

The man hesitated, looking towards the door. "Forget him," said Hope, "if you don't willingly give us this information when you know who this man is, you can be implicated and charged. So please, do yourself a favour and tell us."

The man's head fell. "It's Iain Murdo. He should have been here today."

"Who's Iain Murdo?" asked Hope.

"He's my brother."

Chapter 20

The car raced through the town but Macleod knew he was going to be one of the later arrivals at the house. Hope was driving with due diligence but still pushing the car as quick as she could.

"Iain Murdo Macaulay. Been a member in that church for the last twenty years. Married too. But it seems he has been playing away from home. What is it with these people? I'm sure there's a perfectly normal crowd of people living here but at the moment we keep getting all the randy ones." Macleod shook his head but his chatter was covering a sinking feeling inside. He still had a girl missing and he needed to ensure her safety. It seemed Macaulay was the man after her.

"The uniforms will be there first. Let's hope he was at home," said Hope.

As the car pulled up in front of the town address, Macleod saw the stereotypical Scottish home. Two floors and a grey pebble dash that made sure any drabness inside the house would be reflected on the exterior.

Stepping out of the car, he met a police constable. "Sir, the suspect was not at home but his wife and kids were. PCs Ross and Maclean are interviewing her now. She's not in a great way."

"I'm sure," said Hope, "This is going to be all over the community."

"No, ma'am. He hit her. Badly." The young PC looked at Hope and saw her bruised face. "Even worse than you got it, Ma'am."

"Okay, Constable, thank you. Hope, you go in and see how our uniformed colleagues are doing. Get an address for any friends. Also where does he go on his own? Does he have any lock ups? The usual stuff. I'll make sure Allinson's got the word out to everyone."

"Sir," responded Hope and disappeared inside the front door.

Macleod rang into the station on his mobile but Allinson had everything underway. He was proving to be thorough. Macleod took a piece of paper showing a photocopy of the book in the massage parlour. One of the more expensive accounts had an IM initial with it. *Well that tallies*, he thought, *but there will be another two if I'm not mistaken that will tally with his cohorts from last night.*

"Constable, is the car gone?"

"No, sir. Both family cars are here, his and hers."

"Okay, we need to keep an eye on any stolen vehicles. Call into the station and tell them the murder team want to know if there are any stolen cars reported."

"Yes sir, it'll stand out, we don't tend to get any stolen vehicles here. There's nowhere to go. You'd have to book it on the ferry."

"Good, and car hire?"

"Advised, sir. Going to call us with any new bookings."

It was all being covered, bit by bit. The whole thing seemed open and shut. Macaulay had started seeing Sara and then couldn't let it go. Wanted more than what he paid for. Very neat. Too neat. And then there was the whole cover story for the councillor, one that patently was not true.

Macleod had a feeling the answer was not in the here and now but rather in the past. He still could not get over Sara's tactic of a massage parlour, keeping a boyfriend oblivious to her true feelings for women and yet making money off men when she was not of that persuasion. He couldn't imagine himself entertaining men to make money when he was interested in women. Surely it would work the same the other way round. *Wouldn't it?*

As he looked about the street, he saw the house being sealed off and teams arriving to search it. The day was damp and drizzling now, the earlier bright of the day overtaken by grey cloud and a stickiness closing in. Macleod remembered days like these in summer and of how a mist formed around the harbour. These were days when you had to just get out and about and hope the dreaded midge did not appear, days when you prayed for a little wind.

Hope appeared through the front door of the house and seemed excited. "I think we might know where they are. Apparently he has two buddies, been close since their young days. Angus "flower" Fraser and Donnie Smith, also known as Donnie "Youngs" for some reason. They apparently have a small hut up by Ness on the Westside. Has a boat he takes out sometimes but it's laid up now for repair. Hut belongs to Donnie who's single and a real loner other than with these two. Apparently she was asking him where he'd been last night and got a battering for it."

"Okay, but does she know that's where he has gone?"

"Not for definite," said Hope. "But she did hear him on the mobile and reckoned he was going there."

"Okay, so it's not a definite and it's a fair way away. Take some of the uniforms from here, the big ones that look like they can handle themselves and check it out. That's if you're okay?"

Hope looked at him as if he had asked a daft question. But her face was bruised, deep red in paces, turning purple. And if she felt as sore as he did then it was a more than justified question. "Okay, but look after yourself, let the uniforms take the lead, yes? You're still injured."

Hope nodded but Macleod had the feeling that his ideas might just be ignored. As he watched her rounding up the troops, he was caught up in her positivity and sheer directness. That's how his wife would have been, he was sure of it. Without all the pressure borne on her by this place. Then a thought struck him.

"McGrath, before you go." Hope came over. "How easy is it for a lesbian to be with a man and make it seem normal, in fact as if she's enjoying it?"

Hope stared at him. "How easy would be for you to be with a man?"

"That's what I thought, yet Sara managed it. There's something deeper. I need to do a bit of digging. Go get our man."

Hope nodded and Macleod noted the arrival of Allinson behind her. He also saw the longing look at Hope as she got into her car. *Poor lad*, thought Macleod.

"Allinson, take charge here and ring me with any details. I'm going back to base to search something, okay. Hope's on her way to our man with some heavies. Might be done soon."

Allinson seemed a little surprised but he nodded and headed into the house while Macleod got a lift back to the station from a constable. What was bothering him was the information Hope had given him about Sara's mother and how she had disappeared abroad. If his instincts were right and Sara was somehow conducting a trawl through various men to find someone who had harmed her mother then he would need to find some evidence to back this up. It would certainly give some motive to silence Sara.

Macleod sat in front of the PC and fought hard to search his way through to the case file for Sara's mother. It was a simple entry in many ways, after all she had died whilst abroad so there was little else to be said. But Macleod wanted more, needed to know if there was any rumour around at the time. Something more than a daughter's intuition or wild thoughts. The file showed a DC, who was on secondment at the time, as signing off on the issue and Macleod recognised the name.

Norman Lovett. Four years retired and thank goodness for that. He could not handle the new style of policing, the new style of life, gender equality and all the rest of it. And he had been a bit of a brute too. But not dirty, not dodgy, just very heavy handed. And someone who did not like Macleod with his church background. Still, this was business and the number needed to be called.

Macleod was somewhat apprehensive as the telephone rang but it was a woman's voice that greeted him.

"Hello, this is Detective Inspector Macleod, I'm looking for Norman, would he be available?"

"He'll be available for a drink and that's about it." The woman sounded disgusted.

"It really is quite urgent ma'am, would you have a number I can contact him on?"

"Do you know the Drum on the west side of Glasgow? If

you get their number they might have him. That's where he's been falling over lately. And tell him from me, he can bloody well sleep there in his own shit. If he comes near my bed I'll brain him."

"Thank you, ma'am." And with that Macleod hung up the phone. He knew the pub, he'd seen many a good officer end up in there on a bad day. Macleod was probably one of the few who had ever ordered an orange juice in there without something potent in the glass as well. After checking the database, Macleod found the pub's number and called. A rather dubious sounding individual told him to wait a few moments before a voice he recognised came on.

"Macleod you old shit, what do you want with me? I think I'm a bit beyond your salvation these days."

"Norman, I need your help. About a case you ran up in Stornoway when you were up here."

"For frig's sake man, I can't remember last week let alone ten years ago."

Macleod shook his head at the telephone. "Try. Have a dead girl on my hands. Name of Sara Hewitt. You looked into her mother's death. Died abroad. No body returned. I was wondering was there anything untoward."

"If she was anything like her mother she probably deserved it. I'm sure she was banging different blokes or something. Tasty looker mind from the photographs. But she pissed away off on holiday and didn't come back. Left the wee girl behind with the stepdad. I thought he might have had something funny going on but he was sound. In fact I reckon the mother had been playing away on him. She had a name." Macleod could hear a drink being consumed.

"Anything concrete?"

144

"If there was anything concrete I wouldn't have signed it off as nothing, would I?"

"But any rumours about the mother, like who she was seeing? Who was the other guy?"

A snort came down the telephone. "Guys, frigging hundreds of guys. Like I said, a slapper. But there were other rumours, rumours which in that place were dynamite, especially back then. Not like the dyke friendly days of today."

Macleod rolled his eyes. He struggled with the new genders and openness but it was this sort of abusive thinking that caused the drive for openness.

"You think she had a female lover?"

"That's what they said. Maybe that's what did it, the scandal of being found out. Maybe that's why she went away."

Macleod felt that this would be it, the total sum of information from a drunk man. "Okay Norman, well, I hope retirement's suiting you."

"Retirement, like you give a shit about my retirement. The day we stopped beating the scum on a Saturday night was the day this Police force died, the day…"

Macleod hung up. He recognised the tale that was coming and wanted no part of the obscenities that would no doubt follow. He had an idea but he also had no proof. Looking around the investigation room, he sought someone enterprising. He did not know most of the officers but he decided his intuition would work its magic.

There was a rather chubby faced policewoman at her desk, who seemed to be scanning through a multitude of things on her computer. Anyone that could use these instruments of the devil shone high above others in Macleod's opinion. She would do.

"Officer?"

"Yes!" The officer turned round. "Oh, sorry sir, did not realise it was you. How can I help?"

I need you to trace a death certificate, or at least a letter that informed of the death of a British citizen. Carol Hewitt formerly of here. Her details will be in the case notes from Detective McGrath's visit to her former partner at Ness. She died in Burundi. I need to check up on that, all the paperwork and who signed it through."

"Yes, sir."

"And right now, drop everything else you're doing. Ring me when you've got it all. Okay?"

The officer nodded. Macleod made his way over to the kettle and set it to boil. Staring out the window, he kept running through an idea in his head. Just how clever and how determined was Sara? It seemed beyond his capacity but then his own capacity was no gauge for anyone's.

With the kettle boiled, he poured himself a cup of coffee and then made the officer he had engaged a cup too. Placing it beside her, he smiled, hoping to generate a bit of comforting leadership. Turning back to the window he took a sip of his own coffee. *Poor girl, that tastes like puke.*

Chapter 21

The hut was off the main roads, along a track through a field and then at the sand dunes on the coast. There were not many sand dunes but they were large and full of the soft sand that your feet simply slid through. Hope waved her contingent of uniforms along, surrounding the cabin ahead. It was made of wood and looked like a large shed. Emerging from the top of it was a small, steel chimney which emitted some smoke. The clogging smell of peat reached her nose and she momentarily choked. She was not a fan of real fuel.

The top of the hut was held down by two enormous straps that were gripped to the ground by wooden pegs. She had heard the wind could get up in this part of the world but this seemed ridiculous. Other than the smoke from the chimney, the place seemed deserted but Hope was taking no chances and they surrounded the building.

One of the uniforms knocked the door but there was no answer. Then the rip of a chainsaw cut the air. The door exploded open and knocked the front policeman on the chin causing him to stumble back. The rest retreated quickly seeing the spinning chain coming towards them.

"Police! Halt and put down the chainsaw!" Hope shouted

above the noise but was unsure if she was being heard. Two men emerged from hut, one holding the chainsaw and the other right behind him, a hammer in his hand.

"We're taking our car, stay back and you won't get hurt. But come at me and I'll cut you."

The police formed a loose ring around them as the men moved forward and Hope held her hands up to try and defuse the situation.

"Where are you going to go on an island? The game's up. Put down the chainsaw and hammer and we can talk about this. That's all we need, just the chainsaw and hammer put down."

"Shut it, bitch, I'm in charge, now tell your men to get out of the way." As if to make a point the man with the chainsaw, swung it wildly nearly catching his partner with his follow through.

Hope waved a hand to make her men back off but one stumbled and then fell forward towards the man with the chainsaw. He swung at the constable marking across his back. Hope reacted by racing forward towards the man with the chainsaw. Her colleagues also took action and sought the man with the hammer. As the man with the chainsaw tried to regain his balance, Hope careered into him knocking him to the ground and his hands slipped off the safety of the machine. The incessant whine stopped and she heard him curse.

Rolling to his feet, the man started to run and Hope was on her feet after him. The other officers were subduing the man with the hammer who was intent on putting up a fight. As they raced through the sand dunes, the man ahead realised Hope was gaining and turned towards her. He swung a hard right hand which caught her around the temple. Her face screamed but she rolled with the punch and managed to get two hands on the man. Instinctively she drove a knee hard into his groin. And again. And a third time. He was finished after the first time but this bastard, or one of his mates had nearly broken her jaw in the castle grounds. He deserved a heavily bruised set of family jewels.

She heard her colleagues arriving and she breathed heavily, merely pointing at the man. The sound of handcuffs shutting brought a smile to her face and she indicated they should go back to the cars for questioning.

"Don't forget to bag up that hammer and the chainsaw. Is everyone alright?"

"Anderson's been raked across the back. Not pleasant but not life threatening. We've got the ambulance coming for him," said one of the constables.

Hope nodded and stood for a moment looking out to sea. The waves were rolling in and she thought she could see a kayaker, or maybe a surfer. *This place might be worth a try someday*, she thought.

Walking back to the vehicles, she saw the two men sitting in the back of two different police cars. She decided to try the man with the hammer first and opened the appropriate door.

"Which one are you then? Donnie Youngs?" The man nodded. "Okay, you're looking at assault, maybe even something stronger and possibly attempted murder being out with him last night. So where is he? Tell me where is Macaulay?"

The man shook his head. "I don't know, he said to regroup here after last night. We were going to get a boat, get away to the mainland. But he's shafted us. He's damn well shafted us."

"Why's he want the girl? He was paying Sara Hewitt for sex, wasn't he?"

149

"He was! We were all banging that little hussy. He introduced us, said she was good for it. Nice and quiet too. But with her dead, he said the other girl was going to blame it on us."

"Did you help him kill Sara?"

"Whoa! Hold on. I might rough a few people up but I ain't taking no rap for murder. I might have been rough with her in her room but I ain't done anything like murder. We were just catching her to keep her mouth shut, convince her not to spread lies."

"Station," said Hope, looking at one of the constables. She then spent a few moments with the brute's colleague and found their stories matched up. There would be time to interview them properly but realistically, it seemed that Macaulay had sent them off here to be used as a decoy and the fools had fallen for it. Hope got into her car with one of the constables and drove off back across the track towards the main road.

She turned the corner onto the main road, her mind racing through the questions she would ask the recently apprehended men, the radio of the constable sat in the front seat squawked. She only half heard it. Something about a man near the sea, nearby units requested to assist. Then she heard the word Ness.

The constable slapped the dashboard. "Turn around. Straight back up the road. The main road! It's the harbour behind us."

Hope looked in the rear view mirror, saw a clear piece of road and spun the car around in a quick three point turn. She could hear a siren in the air now, most probably one of the police cars ahead of them on the return trip. Her foot close to the floor, she negotiated the narrow road out to the harbour. On parking, her colleague was out first and running towards the end of the harbour wall where a woman with a dog was pointing into the sea.

"He's out there," shouted the woman. "He just jumped in. I told him to be careful but he walked right off the pier. Oh God, he walked right in."

Hope ran past the increasingly hysterical woman and looked out into what was a mild surf. Sure there was a swell but she had seen much worse even on the west coast of the mainland. The constable was talking into his radio, confirming with control there was a person in the water and requesting assistance from the coastguard and lifeboat.

Any assistance was going to take time, thought Hope and she looked around for anything she could use to help the man in the water. She saw the red casing of a life ring cabinet and ran for it, opening it quickly and removing the life saving device. With precision, she threw the ring right beside the man in the water who was just about above water. It floated on top of the sea and its momentum caused it to hit the man in the side. He put a hand onto it and seemed to float with it for a few moments.

But Hope saw a face that was not in panic. It was solemn, almost calm. As she heard the noise of other vehicles arriving behind her, she almost began to drift into a moment that seemed out of time. Did the man smile? Did he look relieved? And then he simply let go of the life ring. In a moment he had submerged and the ring continued to float.

Hope scanned the surface, desperately looking for the man but nothing appeared. "He was there, right there, she shouted at the constable. As she continued to scan the water, time seemed to pass slowly. It seemed an age before a helicopter arrived on scene. There were men and women in blue overalls and lifejackets arriving onto the pier. Hope pointed, said what happened, but inside she felt her heart sinking.

A coastguard gently moved her away from the edge of the pier, saying that they had it now. The noise around her became a blur as she sat down on the bonnet of the police car. Her body turned numb and she could not feel the breeze about her. Even when a drizzle began, she did not register the cooling mist of water. But in her mind was a face.

He had smiled. He had definitely smiled. Like a release, as if this was his cure to everything, a journey completed. She had gotten the life ring to him. As she lifted her head, she could see the ring still out there in the water. Presently, someone came and told her she had done well, that the ring was showing them where he would drift. But they still had not seen him.

An hour later and the man had not been sighted. There was a helicopter overhead and a lifeboat on scene, as well as a contingent of coastguards and many police. Hope had not moved and her blouse was now wet and she could feel the chill in her bones. Her mobile was ringing, vibrating in her pocket and she took it out. It was a temporary one and she did not recognise the number. Answering she heard a voice she recognised.

"McGrath, I'm about to go in with our two men you grabbed at Ness, are you nearly done up there or should I take someone else in?" asked Macleod.

Hope did not answer. She shivered and held the phone to her ear but she did not speak. Her eyes drifted back to the piece of water where the man had been. It had not changed, the water still giving that constant, almost swaying motion.

"Hope, are you there?"

"I saw him go under," she blurted.

"The man at the pier. You were that close."

"Yes," she blurted and then bent over double as a wave of anger ran through her. She snorted as she cried, tears streaming. Someone grabbed her and put an arm around her. She could hear Macleod calling her name on the phone before someone took it off her and explained to him.

Eventually she stood up and walked away from the pier back to the road they had raced down only an hour earlier. Cold and numb, she just wanted away from the scene. A constable intercepted her.

"Detective, that car over there is going back to the station. Let them take you back."

Hope nodded and allowed herself to be steered towards the correct car. As it made its way along the road back to Stornoway, across moor and the sight of the large wind turbines stationary today in the light breeze, she saw the man's face again. He smiled. Maybe he was happy now. What could make you smile like that?

She emerged from the car at the station and as she entered the building, she saw Macleod looking towards her with concern. He came up to her and wrapped his arms around her. Hope said nothing but her shock at what had happened must have been obvious. She was seated in a quiet office, Macleod handing her a cup of tea and just letting her sit there. Gradually she told him, taking time over everything. Detailing the life ring, the man's hand touching it and then the smile. Over and over again, she mentioned the smile.

He had said one phrase and it had made her snap to the present. He had said it as he left the room, but there were tears in his eyes as he had. It was after mentioning that his wife had walked out into the sea too. His body had shaken as he said it

153

and she saw Seoras falling apart under the strain of telling her. Now standing in the shower, letting the warm water bring her chilled body back to life, she felt for him in a way she could not have before the events of the day.

Just one phrase, but it was ringing in her head over and over again. *She smiled too.*

Chapter 22

Macleod watched Hope enter the room and tried to assess her fitness for the job from her face. It was not a prescribed method but he did not have many senior officers and he needed her right now. He had been discussing the case with Allinson while waiting for Hope to come back from the hotel. Given her state and physical condition, he thought the best thing was to start again and had sent her back to the hotel for a few hours to sleep and change. In the meantime, he had conducted the interviews with Youngs and Fraser, both feeling suitably stitched up by Macaulay.

At Macaulay's prompting, they had become involved with Sara Hewitt, paying for her services in the bed above the massage parlour. Thoroughly unpleasant individuals, Macleod had felt anger at their using of the girl and the more this case unravelled he was beginning to see a dark side that went far beyond what he had encountered when he had lived here. But the main question he had for the men had gone unanswered. Macaulay was missing, on the run. They had not seen him since they had come back from their adventures in the castle grounds when they had encountered Macleod and tried to capture the young woman.

"McGrath," shouted Macleod over the noise of the investigation room. Hope made her way over to them and Macleod watched her smile. It seemed reasonably forced but it was good to see her fighting. Her face still had the marks from the punches she had taken in the castle grounds, ruining an otherwise smooth face but the deep purple almost blended in with her red hair, once again tied up in a ponytail.

"I was just running through with Allinson where we should be looking for Macaulay. I also sent a car out for Marie Smith, as I think we need to talk again to our Councillor."

He watched Hope nod and sit down on the edge of a table. He had prayed that she could shake the incident at Ness off and get on with the next few days as if nothing had happened but he knew that had been a forlorn wish. He'd have to watch her over the next few days.

"We've got a check on all the normal routes off the island and have a warning out at the smaller harbours but it's difficult to close the net tight. There are too many out of the way places to lock it tight."

"The boss is right," said Allinson, "it would be easy to jump aboard a yacht or dinghy, or even a motor vessel. It's summer so we can't simply stop them from being here, and we can't check them all."

"Is he going to run?" asked Hope. "I mean off the island. And are we sure it's him that killed Sara? What do we have actually linking him to it? He was after her friend, a witness to what? She didn't see a killer, she only knew the dirty secrets. Yes, he's at the scene but that's all."

"He's not exactly coming forward," said Macleod, "not really the actions of an innocent man."

A plain clothes officer approached Allinson and handed him

a piece of paper which he read with apparent interest. There was a small shake of the head before he spoke.

"The incident up at Ness. We still haven't found a body but there seems little doubt it's McKinney, Marie Smith's supposed lover. He's been missing from his home since church this morning and the woman who saw him go in has identified him."

"Marie Smith. Get the car we sent out and found out if they have her." Macleod was raging inside. The guy had been stitched up to cover the councillor and obviously did not have the stomach to carry out these games that were being played. Looking up, he saw Hope staring away at a wall. "Allinson, go check out if they have found her."

When Allinson had moved out of earshot, Macleod moved closer to Hope. "It won't go away today. It probably won't go away in a week, and it may even never leave you fully. But I need you now, right here in this room and with that brain in full gear. I want to say fly back to Glasgow and take some time but I think things are about to heat up further."

Hope turned her head and looked at him, sullen eyes almost tipping into tears. Macleod reached up with a hand and placed it on her cheek. Looking at her reminded him of that day, and part of him was wishing that this woman he had thought of as loose and wild when he had seen her at the Glasgow station would just disappear. But another part wanted to see her back to her former glory, restored to full fitness, mentally and physically. Something he could not do for his wife.

"I'll be okay. I'm good," said Hope.

She wasn't and Macleod understood the professional in-tegrity of saying you will soldier on. "You're not, but you'll have to do. If it gets too much, then I'm here. Okay? We'll get you a world of counsellors afterwards but in the here and now, I'm here." He saw her nod. "Okay, let's find our man, our young woman and this blasted councillor."

Allinson was returning and cast a glance at Macleod which asked if it was okay to re-enter the conversation. Macleod nodded and sat back again but his eyes were still on Hope.

"She's not at her house," said Allinson, "nor is she at her son's. The neighbour said she disappeared about four hours ago, walking out, leaving her car."

"She's got a bus then," said Hope.

"Not here," replied Allinson, "no buses on a Sunday."

"Then she's either on foot, or a taxi," surmised Macleod. "Get someone onto the taxi companies, see if they had a fare close to there or a call to somewhere unusual. Of course she could have just gone to a rank. Hire car firms too, get on to them and check if anyone paid cash or if she's actually been daft enough to use her own name."

Allinson nodded and turned away to issue instructions when a female constable walked straight up to Macleod and handed him some paper. "The detail you asked for sir, regarding the Carol Hewitt case. I have nothing to say she ever left the country and nothing to say she actually died out there except for a tour operator's report. I have rung through the contacts at the tour operator and no one remembers anything about this. It's like it just didn't happen."

"Sir?" questioned Hope.

"Carol Hewitt, Sara's mother died while on holiday after she took off from her partner without notice. I thought I'd make sure that story was accurate and as of now I cannot collaborate the story at all. We've been checking the tour company and no one remembers a death or a funeral out there at that time.

158

A former colleague who ran the small investigation into this also believed that Carol was a rather promiscuous individual and was involved with others. I'm beginning to think the past has a lot more to do with this."

"The men," said Hope, "you're thinking that Sara might have been doing some investigating in her own way about this. That would explain why she changed her tune with her stepdad. But what did she know? What got her killed?"

Macleod shrugged his shoulders. "Did she find the truth? Or was she just too close for comfort? Either way, we need Macaulay and Smith as there's too many questions left that I need answers for. And I think they can give me those answers."

Hope slipped off the edge of the desk she was sitting on. "Key thing is to find our girl first before whoever gets to her. I'm going to run over to her house again, in case we missed anything. Where is she hiding? After all she's been off radar in a place like this."

Macleod smiled. Hope's sudden perking up was good news, and he was not going to curb her ideas. "Good. Let me know if you find anything."

He watched her turn and walk off and realised Allinson was watching her too. A wave of tiredness swept over Macleod and he found himself just staring at Hope leaving. Her figure was certainly pleasing but there was something else as well. *Well, everything's bound to be scrambled up in my head with all that's happening,* he thought. But he did not stop staring until he saw her turn the corner out of the investigation room.

Wearily, Macleod turned back to the team in the investigation room. They were buzzing away on different jobs, a hive of activity, and a prime example for himself. But he was feeling bruised and battered. Sleep had not been plentiful in recent days and the bruising from the scrap in the castle grounds was telling on him. Unlike Hope, he seemed to feel the damage a lot more. But then she was young and he was past his prime. At least physically.

Standing at a wall which housed the photo board from the investigation, Macleod gave the impression he was standing and staring in deep thought. As long as the rest of the team believed this he could take a break. His eyes did not see the pictures before him and his only real sensation was when he felt the warm liquid of the coffee run down his throat.

Although his eyes were not registering anything, his mind was on a long sandy beach watching a woman enter such perfectly clear water. Running away from him, she splashed into the water only to shriek and then turn and run back toward him. His eyes swept her bikini clad body, before he ran forward and swept her up in his arms, charging back into the surf and throwing both of them under the water. Rising up he looked into the eyes of the woman he was holding and spoke two words.

Luskentyre beach had been where she had said yes. Maybe he needed to get to a better memory. When this was all over he would take a few days and try and piece back some happier times on the islands.

"Sir, we believe Marie Smith may have hired a van. One of the team was checking through and the clerk at the car hire said it was last minute and matched her description. However the name's wrong. They are sending over a scan of her signature that we can match to some council paperwork to see if it's accurate."

"Good work, Allinson. But where is she going to go? And who for?" asked Macleod. It was clear that Marie Smith and

160

Macaulay were the main players in this game but how it all fitted was just beyond him. His mobile vibrated in his pocket. From habit he looked at the number but it meant nothing.

"Macleod?"

"Sir, it's Hope. I've been looking through the young woman's stuff and there's a photo album here with a lot of pictures of Sara. She's in a den of some sort with green vegetation around it. I'd don't recognise any of it but I'm going to bring it back. One thing I do see in it is that she has a sort of keepsake box. In a few photos her lover has it."

"Where was the photo album?" asked Macleod.

"Stored away, sir. But not in the sense of being archived as the access to it had been opened recently and it was separate to the other photo albums. Seems they liked their pictures."

"Get back here with it. Maybe Allinson and the team can tell us where it's from."

"On my way but there's something else, sir. At the rear of the album there's pictures of a lot of men. I recognise three of them, Macaulay, Youngs and Fraser. There's also Marie Smith. I'm sure the photos are from the upstairs at the massage parlour. There's nothing candid about them but the subjects look unaware."

Macleod waved a hand at Allinson who was talking to a colleague across the room. "Okay, McGrath, get back over here." Closing the call on the mobile, Macleod looked up to see Allinson arrive before him.

"McGrath's found some pictures of a possible location for our young woman. I want your best people for knowing your locations and get them in a room. Where she returns, I'll get McGrath to show them all the photos, and then I need a place. This may be what we need to understand what's going on. So

161

get me your best, Allinson."

Allinson smiled, "Yes, sir." With a bounce in his step he set off to talk to different people in the room and Macleod watched his renewed vigour. He should have been feeling this pick-up himself but inside he was still thinking of Luskentyre. It started at the water and at the water it ended. It dawned on him that since leaving the island for Glasgow he had never gone to the beach. Maybe he should have because for years her body, poorly covered by her bikini, in the cold water had never come to mind.

Chapter 23

Macleod waited outside the rear entrance to the station, taking in some fresh air, glad to step out from the stuffy rooms inside. Sometimes it was hard to concentrate when the rooms got hot, an issue caused by the sheer amount of people working hard in a small space. But the industry shown was pleasing to him. It would not be a lack of effort that let this investigation down.

The door behind him opened and Allinson drew up to his shoulder. The man's tie was now loosened and his top collar button undone. There was an impatience in the man, a need to get going which pleased Macleod. You never quite knew how more remote stations would be, or what resources they really had. But then again, Stornoway was hardly a village, a population of at least ten thousand in the town and surrounding area, over twenty thousand in the Outer Hebrides. And things seemed to be changing here, despite his memories.

"She should be here any minute, sir. I have them assembled in the annex room, maps and paper, ready to go," said Allinson. Macleod noticed he was hoping from foot to foot, not in an exaggerated form but he was doing it. *Maybe he should go in and give the team a pep talk before they looked at the pictures. No, they know what to do. And what would he say? Look carefully?*

Rack your brains? No, they knew this was important, a good shot at catching up with the missing woman. Let them work.

"You've done well, Allinson, been a great help. But let's get this closed."

"Of course, sir. And thank you. Been good working with you. And with McGrath also, be sorry to see you go."

It was the right thing to say but Macleod could tell who he was really sorry to see leave. But Hope was proving more complex than he had initially thought. The reputation did not match the woman, or at least not in the way he thought it would. You would have thought as a detective he might have guessed that.

The unmarked car drove into the car park and stopped in an empty bay. A long leg in jeans emerged followed by a loose blouse and then the swinging red ponytail. As Hope walked towards them, Macleod realised that the men were both staring, like a pair of dogs waiting for their master. Time to show a bit of professionalism.

"Well done, McGrath, let's see them."

Hope handed over an envelope, and Macleod took out the photos inside, flicking through them quickly. There were close ups of men in the upper room, Marie Smith too. And there were other locations, or maybe it was the same one. But Sara showed in these, stretched out, or sitting up smiling. The whole feel of the photos changed from a feel of evidence to that of a lover's record as the scenery changed. Sara had certainly been a looker. And she had used those looks to draw in so many.

Macleod handed the pictures to Allinson. "Go." As Hope went to follow Allinson, Macleod placed a hand on her arm stopping her. "Wait a moment."

"Sir?"

"How are you doing?" asked Macleod.

"It helps to stay busy. My jaw is stinging, hurts when I chew and I swear I have new bruises I didn't know about." Hope forced a smile.

"I meant upstairs. The incident at Ness. I saw something similar in Glasgow but I was a few minutes behind. The man had already gone under and we never saw him for two months when he suddenly washed up. It's hard with no resolution, no understanding."

"Yeah, it is. But I need to work. When we're done, I'll get on a plane, find a beach in the sun and get my bikini on and soak up some rays, and then let it all drift away with some ridiculous sized cocktail. You should join me, looking at you."

Macleod laughed. "I don't do summer shorts well." *But it would be so nice*, he thought.

"Yeah, maybe not," said Hope. She walked inside and Macleod was left looking at the quiet car park.

I haven't had a holiday since she left me, either. Maybe that's what I need, some time away, some beach with a set of stupid looking shorts, some sun and someone like Hope to talk to and look at. Would that be so wrong, God? Let these guys find something before it's too late.

Following his team inside, Macleod stood at the door of the annexe, watching the feverish activities of the people inside. Allinson had separated the photos and had placed all those being pictures of Sara and her lover to one end of the table. At the other end pictures of the people who had been in the upstairs room were being identified.

Allinson watched Hope slide in amongst the team, casting a cautious eye across proceedings. There was excitement

165

and questions flying back and forth about possible locations. Magnifying glasses were being used on some photos to try and spot anything in the background that could be something. A couple of computers were at the edge of the room, set on freely available mapping systems from the internet and one policeman was already finding a road and then getting the local image to try and tally it to a photograph.

Macleod watched the man shake his head and knew how he felt. So much of police work was a dead end. It was like an endurance test, piecing things together and then when you did, it turns out it has nothing to do with anything and you pick up the next strand. But he had a good feeling about this. Which in truth meant, he had no other options other than a needle being found from the roadside questioning still going on.

After twenty minutes of standing and watching, Macleod left the room and instead entered the investigation room. The room was quieter than usual but was still over half full. His arrival meant heads popped up over computers and he got several nods to acknowledge his presence. He smiled back but noticed one young policewoman was intense on the telephone. When she hung up the call, she waved Macleod over.

"That was the Coastguard, sir. There's been a body washed up on rocks at Ness. It's McKinney, sir. Positive I.D. from one of the Coastguards who knew him. We are getting the formalities done but it's him."

Macleod nodded and thanked the policewoman. Although he knew it was coming, the finality of finding a body after someone was already believed dead still gave him a jolt. It was like he could never believe and always sought that final chance that an escape was made. But it never was.

Another voice called him and he was directed to an office to take a telephone call from his boss in Glasgow. He always found her honest and straight, which is why he managed to accept her being so high up the organisation. Her mind was never that great when it came to detective work but then again that was not her role now. She did not get involved in the nitty gritty of crime but rather looked with a different view, dealing with the statistics, the budgets and the public perceptions.

"So, this is touch and go, Macleod. Do you need any more resources?"

"No, Ma'am. I doubt that by the time they get here they will be of any use. We need to know where to search. This will be one by brainwork rather than footwork."

"Have you given any press briefings? I saw Allinson giving general statements but none from you."

Macleod hated press briefings but they had to be done. Unless of course you looked like you had been kicked to pieces such as Hope and himself looked at the moment.

"I'm a little worse for wear after getting a beating when we rendezvoused with the woman. McGrath looks worse. She's going to need some recovery when we're done. She saw the man at Ness go down. It's right there with her but she's keeping going with the investigation. Once we're done it'll all flood back at her."

His boss continued and Macleod discussed about when the press would be briefed of what and if it was worth putting out calls. When he had hung up, he returned to the investigation room.

"Sir," called a police woman to him. It was the same one who had been working the angle about Carol Hewitt's overseas death. "We have the scan of Marie Smith's council documents and the hire form for the rental van. They are very similar in style. Look," she said throwing two pieces of paper down before him. "The style is the same though the name's different. Points to being her."

"Good, as we thought," replied Macleod.

"But there's more, sir. Look at this document from the travel company from when Carol Hewitt died. The signature, sir. It's the same fluid style. I'd say it's the same writer. But that's ridiculous as this is from a travel company."

"No," said Macleod, "it's not ridiculous at all. You just confirmed my suspicions. Get a hand writing expert onto this, just to confirm it properly, but you're right. Excellent work. Just excellent."

There was a buzz in Macleod's step as he returned to the annexe, but inside there was also a dread. If Carol Hewitt was actually disposed of rather than simply died on holiday, then there was a past to hide as well as a present. He needed a place to go to, he needed to know the woman's hideout.

"Sir," said Hope as he entered, "we have a possibility. It's near a loch side and there's no great access to it."

"Is it definite?" asked Macleod.

"No, but we believe it's at least an eighty percent chance of being the place. We're trusting one of the team's memories from two years ago but the spot is remote. If you look at this photo and see the slight piece of beach at the edge. Well that coupled with the corner of a rock structure here in this photograph and this hollow, here in this photograph, makes our man believe he knows where it is."

Macleod struggled to follow the logic and deduction but frankly did not care. After all that was why he had brought them through here, for their local knowledge. "So let's roll there."

"That's the thing, sir. It's about a three hour walk across moorland. It really is out of the way. We could get a helicopter over to look and see."

"There's the Coastguard helicopter up here, try it," suggested Allinson.

Macleod nodded. The arrival might be noisy but at least if the woman ran they would see her. He told Allinson to contact the Coastguard and then waved Hope over to him. Detailing the findings over the travel company and rental van, Macleod told Hope his theory. "I reckon Carol Hewitt was killed and put aside and I believe Marie Smith was involved in some way. You said Marie Smith preferred women. And she was with Sara, so is it possible that she was also involved with Carol. Back then being outed would have been catastrophic."

"Possible, said Hope, "but it doesn't change what we do. Find this site, find the woman, and keep her safe.

As they waited for Allinson to come back, Macleod felt a growing dread. McKinney had been pressured to his death, Carol Hewitt seemed to be murdered and her daughter certainly had been. Three killings to cover whatever up. The killer would presumably not stop if they felt threatened.

"The helicopter is away on a job. But I've gotten the lifeboat to help. It's just round the corner, sir, we need to go now," said Allinson.

"Good," replied Macleod, "Allinson, get someone to show us the way and a few more. McGrath, you're with me. Allinson, keep everything running here. And don't let up on the rental van search, we need to find it and Marie Smith."

Within ten minutes, Macleod was standing at the door of the lifeboat station and shaking the hand of the cox of the vessel. He was taken inside and kitted up with a life jacket before being led with his team to the range vessel on the pontoons at Stornoway harbour. He had never been on a lifeboat before and was surprised by the size of it and the multitude of screens and controls. After being strapped in at the rear of the front cockpit, he waited for the vessel to depart and they went slow until they cleared Stornoway harbour. The Severn class lifeboat then opened up its engines and Macleod was glad he was strapped in. As they bounced through the waves, a crewman advised Macleod on the location of a sick bag, in case he needed it.

"Don't worry," said the man, "there's no embarrassment, everyone gets sick on here at some point."

It took over thirty minutes to arrive at the right inlet and then to route along it to the beach in the photographs. The beach itself was obvious, the small sandy cove sticking out from the rocks and moorland behind it. As the vessel bounded towards the land, Macleod found it hard to focus and looked across at Hope who was gripping a stanchion.

The cox shouted back from his seat at the front. "There's something on the beach, sir. We can't go that close but we can launch the Y-boat out to the shore. But I don't want my crew going ashore if there's going to be violence. We're not trained for that sort of thing."

"Of course not, sir," said Macleod. "Can you get a few of us onto the beach? I'm happy for your crew to remain in the boat until we make sure it's safe. If they stay in the water but close, in case we need to retreat."

The cox nodded and as they brought the lifeboat close, the crew prepared the smaller boat at the rear of the vessel. Macleod and Hope were deposited into the boat and with two crew they made their way to the beach. As they got closer, Macleod could see red stains beside a body. It was a large figure, a male figure. As the boat reached the sandy shore, Hope jumped out from the boat ahead of him and ran up to the body. Macleod was somewhat clumsier and by the time he had cleared the water Hope was already beside the man.

"It's Macaulay, sir, and he's been cut across his throat, and a lot more afterwards."

Macleod looked around but there was no one else. He saw some remains of a campfire, some empty tins of food, as if someone had been here. But no sign of the woman. *Damn!*

Chapter 24

Hope was walking around the makeshift camp site looking for anything that might help. Watching her from the water's edge, Macleod was observing slumped shoulders and a touch of dejection that was far from the woman who had leapt out of the boat. The mobile phone did not work here and Macleod had relayed instructions via the lifeboat and the Coastguard back to Allinson who should be organising some vessels and more officers to reach the site.

Tucked away in a small loch, the beach site had a small area of sand and then a rocky ledge leading up to a small patch of moorland. The ground seemed difficult for Macleod saw Hope stumble a few times. Walking the shoreline, Macleod looked for any marks or indications of another boat having beached but the sand was perfect. There were also no footprints near the water except for the mess they had made coming ashore.

A crewman had thrown up on seeing the corpse and Macleod stepped around the sickly mess that was touching the tide. The poor guy was still in a touch of shock and Macleod had suggested he return to the lifeboat and they get someone else to shuttle the remaining officers onto the beach. With the last of the officers now ashore, the two-person crew in the small boat were sat on the beach trying to look elsewhere.

"Sir," shouted Hope.

Macleod looked around and then spotted her red hair up on the grass beyond the beach. He skirted well around the body and clambered up to the grass area where he saw Hope pointing into a gap in the rock face beyond. Joining her, he let her take the lead in getting onto her knees and entering the small gap in the rocks. Watching her trim backside disappear, he wondered how deep this entry into the rock face was and got onto his knees to follow Hope.

The entry was dark inside and he saw a single, small, directed light ahead beyond his colleague. But he could see little else and proceeded slowly, hands out in front, checking for loose rock or jutting pieces. The space to crawl in was narrow and Macleod had his head down feeling his way along. Then his head banged into the backside he had seen disappear inside and his hands reached forward to ascertain the lie of the cave. Unfortunately his hand rested briefly on Hope's rear before he could work out there was a severe lack of space.

"There's a den up here of sorts," said Hope, ignoring his scrabbling hands, "and there's some roll mats, all jammed together. A rucksack and a notebook. A thick one. Come up and see."

Hope flashed the torch down at her body as she forced herself to one side of the tiny cave. Macleod saw the tight gap ahead and wormed his way forward but could not help brushing up to his colleague the whole way. It felt unseemly and he could smell her subtle perfume this close. It was a delicate scent and extremely pleasant but he tried to focus on the task ahead. As his face met inches from Hope's face, she swung round the torch leaving them in darkness and illuminating the small area ahead.

173

The rucksack against the wall looked full. Some crumbs of food and a few empty cans of a cheap beer were also lying crushed up. But there were photos stuck onto the wall above the little den. Sweet, almost innocent photos of Sara and her lover together, arm in arm or wrapped in each other.

"This was their place then," said Hope. "I guess they could come here and be themselves away from other people."

"Yes but they brought someone else here, or else how did Macaulay get here? Someone told him about it, set him up and I reckon it's Marie Smith. They brought Marie Smith out here at some point."

"No," replied Hope, "not to here, it's too precious. She made Marie pay for sex. This is not the place you would bring someone like that. There's something wrong in that theory."

Macleod tried to reach forward for the notebook beside the rucksack and slipped from his delicate balance down into Hope resting up against her in a rather compromised position. Realising he had gotten himself into a poor position he quickly apologised and tried to adjust but that only made his position even closer so he could feel her body touching his.

"If this wasn't the middle of a murder case, this would be funny," said Hope. She let out an inadvertent giggle.

Macleod let a wry laugh go as well. "I'm going to extract myself," he advised, "and then if you bring out the rucksack and the notebook, we'll see if there's anything of importance in there. Get a photo first of course. Do you have any gloves?"

"No," said Hope, "I didn't put any in when I changed. Have you?"

"Yes," said Macleod, "in my left trouser pocket, which I'm lying on." He tried to shift and although his trouser pocket came out from under him, he also shifted again finding his nose touching Hope's. "I'll get out and throw them in, shall I?"

"I've a free arm," said Hope and Macleod felt a hand working down his chest and then tracing a line to his trousers before a hand rummaged inside and pulled out some gloves. In his mind he was laughing at the ridiculousness of the situation. Not since his wife had he been this close to a woman, so close the bodies really touched, at several parts. And that smell up close, it was intoxicating. *I need to get out*, he thought, *but I missed this. She really is...* Macleod left his thoughts and decided to move. Getting out produced another farce of positioning and when he accidentally placed a hand on her bottom in trying to go backwards, Hope actually joked she thought he was doing this deliberately. He prayed he was not.

Adjusting himself as he exited the cave, Macleod stood and looked again on the scene around him. Macaulay still lay on the beach, his throat slashed. So if Marie Smith had come here, how did she know and what was her aim? The young woman was not here. Did Marie Smith find Macaulay? Did she set him up? Was the young woman here and Smith now has her?

"Sir, can you grab the bag?" Hope's feet were sticking out of the cave entrance and a small brown rucksack emerged past them. Taking the bag and setting it behind him, Macleod knelt by the entrance and then received a notebook from Hope. He waited until she had back peddled herself out far enough to accept a hand and pull herself up.

"Tight in there. But cosy if it's the person you want to be with," said Hope. "I could imagine it being a sweet escape from the world, way out here and somewhere to cuddle up with the storms outside."

"Yes, of course," replied Macleod. *I can still smell the perfume.* He turned away and knelt down with the notebook opening it

175

up on a nearby rock. He really had missed the closeness.

With the notebook open, he flipped through the pages. Inside were a few pictures he recognised. One had Macaulay asleep on a bed. The colour of the covers matched the duvet spread in the upstairs apartment of the massage parlour. There were pictures of Macaulay's associates too. Again asleep on the bed. There were others too. Men of an older age, never looking younger than around forty.

"A customer record for bribery?" asked Hope.

"An investigative log, McGrath. She was looking for a middle aged man. I think she was sleeping with men to find out more about them. Looking for a certain kind of person. One who having bedded her mother a long time ago would then fancy the daughter. It's sick."

"But effective. She tracked her man. He killed her."

"No, Hope, she killed her." Macleod kept turning the pages until he came across the sleeping face of Marie Smith. "I'm not sure Sara Hewitt actually knew but she suspected her involvement. Hence she took her as a paying client."

Hope blew out a sigh. "You'd have to be so driven to sleep with people you thought might have had something to do with your Mother's disappearance."

"Yes you would, but she learnt something of that from her mother I presume. It seems she played about a bit. I wonder how much Sara really knew before she died." Macleod had seen this young woman as a slut, a promiscuous woman who did what she wanted for her own gain. But now he saw the driven vehicle of righteousness seeking what had happened to her mother, doing whatever to achieve that.

"Do you think our young woman was here?" asked Hope.

"No. Or at least she never revealed herself. If she did I would think she'd be dead and a tableau set up to have us believe Macaulay killed her. I doubt Smith thought we would know about this place. And when someone did stumble across it, the young girl could be blamed."

"Unless that's the point," said Hope. "If our young woman was here and Marie Smith has taken her. If the young woman disappears and Macaulay is found, then Smith would be off the hook as we would think the girl did it. Probably in self-defence when Macaulay attacked her. Maybe she has her, boss."

"And needs to get rid of her quietly. That's a possibility, definitely, we have to check it. And she never saw this notebook, or the bag. Or at least I doubt it. She'd have removed herself from it surely. Maybe."

"What she did or didn't know can wait, sir. If I'm right…"

"Yes, McGrath. Let's get back to the lifeboat and get moving, I need to contact Allinson. If Marie Smith came here I doubt it was on foot. She's not strong enough to carry someone out to the road, it's miles away. But she did take a hire car. So where did she go?"

"The lifeboat, let's ask the coxswain, he'll know the area."

Together they strode back to the small y-boat and called to the crewmen on board to fetch them back. Macleod could see the younger crewman turning away from the sight of Macaulay on the beach. The other, however, was in a state of fascination. Macleod's shoes and ankles got soaked as he boarded as did those of Hope. The younger crewman perked up from his rejection of the beach scene as he helped her aboard, sitting directly behind her.

Once back on board the lifeboat, Macleod asked to speak to the cox and detailed Hope's idea that someone may have been taken off the beach by someone else.

"Where would they go and what sort of vessel would you need? Where would they tie up and meet up with a vehicle?"

"Let's look at the charts," the man replied and took them within the cockpit to the screen plotter, the electronic charts that sat in front of the vessel's navigator. Macleod stared without understanding as the cox and his navigator looked along what Macleod presumed were shorelines. The cox then turned to Macleod, "well, they could take a small rhib or dinghy and put alongside at a number of these little slipways. But someone would probably see them.

"We can take a run along but you don't know what you're looking for. If I was going for inconspicuous, I wouldn't be landing at any of these little slipways, we have fishermen using them most days. You could ask the Coastguard to put out a broadcast but it would be so vague. I can call them and see if they have had any strange reports around here."

"Please do." Macleod turned back to Hope, his face giving a frustrated air as he bit his bottom lip.

"Sir?"

"Needle in a haystack. The Cox says there's a few slipways but they are pretty active and unlikely to have been used."

"She would need to hide out, maybe? Somewhere abandoned? Maybe not a large slipway, but somewhere where you could get the boat off the water," said Hope.

The cox interrupted. "Detective, the Coastguard have had nothing unusual reported. I suggest we route a little further down the loch and see what we can find. Maybe there's something I'm missing."

"Again, please do," said Macleod.

"If you'd join me up top, we can get a better view. This way, please." The Cox pointed the way out of the cockpit to the rear door of the craft and Macleod followed Hope out onto the rear deck. From there, the Cox took them up a small ladder onto the upper open deck where Macleod saw another set of steering apparatus and further controls.

"Hang on to something with one hand at all times," said the Cox. "Might get bumpy."

Macleod held on with two hands as the vessel swung away down the loch. His eyes glanced over at Hope who was standing like she had been on a boat all her life. Her eyes scanned the shore and Macleod decided to join her scan rather than keep looking at her.

He felt vulnerable, like a rawness inside was exposed. The memories of the horror he endured at his wife's death had brought up unexpected memories of intimacy in their life that he was struggling to keep down. And Hope kept bringing them to the surface every time he looked at her. *Dear God, what is this? Give me control, I don't need this now.*

And then he heard a voice. It penetrated through the splash of the boat cutting the waves. It was clear through the roar of the engines and the wind rushing past him. *Yes you do*, it said.

The lifeboat tore along the loch which began to narrow. The Cox had been right and they had seen a few slipways which had small boats attached and they could have been used. Having seen Macaulay's corpse, he had to have been dead for maybe more than six hours. Macleod needed men here in boats to go and question any loch workers or those that lived around her. But that would take time and that was not something they had the luxury of.

"What's that?" shouted Hope above the waves.

"Arracaig House," shouted the Cox, "abandoned maybe twenty years. Was a pretty house in its day but now just a ruin."

"Can we get close?" asked Macleod.

"Sure." The Cox took the lifeboat in close to the shore but stopped a little away. "I have to be careful here, don't want to ground the lifeboat, they're kind of expensive."

Macleod watched the man smile at Hope as he said this. She had a way of bringing out the little flirtations men have.

"There!" shouted a crewwoman.

"Where, Anna?"

"Behind the bank with the weeds. I can see red, possible side of a dinghy. Not sure but it looks like it."

"Can we get in there?" asked Macleod.

"Aye, in the y-boat, Detective."

"Then please, as quickly as you can."

A few minutes later, Macleod and Hope were with their two crewmen and heading for the sighting in the y-boat. As they got close Hope jumped out onto the bank and scrambled for the bank of weeds.

"Yes, it's a boat alright. Got a small outboard on it. There's some blood in it too."

Macleod scrambled onto the bank, his feet sodden as he had inadvertently stepped into the water when he jumped out. "Is it fresh?"

Hope nodded and Macleod turned to look at the ruin that was Arracaig House. He hoped he was not too late.

Chapter 25

Macleod motioned to the lifeboat crewmen to stay at the y-boat and joined Hope at the small dinghy she had found. There was blood on the boat but it was deposited by hands wiping as opposed to drops having been spilled. Still, it was not a good sign and Macleod indicated to Hope that they should make for the house he could see beyond the dinghy.

There was a faint path through the moorland towards the house which stood like a grey bastion in the spongy surroundings. From his lower vantage point, Macleod could not see any roads or paths and decided to strike out as directly as he could for the building. His feet became covered in moss and that purple heather that seemed to surround the moor. Despite it being summer, he still felt a chill in his feet and had to force himself forward.

Due to the difficulty in maintaining his footing, Macleod only glanced up at the building sporadically but he failed to see anyone at the windows. He knew anyone inside would see them coming from afar but there was no time to be stealthy, and no other way he could see across the moor. As his foot slipped down into the heather again, he felt a tap on his shoulder.

"Sir, just across from us, the heather has been pushed down a bit, like something's been dragged across it."

Staring at the patch of ground, Macleod concurred and then dragged his foot back out of the moor. He tried to quicken his pace but tripped and fell face first into the spongy, wet mass. An arm swung under his and helped pull him up.

"Stick to firmer patches. In fact I'll go first. Just follow me." Hope stepped across in front of him and he found himself watching her feet, seeing them plant firmly on more solid terrain. Her long legs stretched at times in her jeans to a size of step he struggled with. Once she stopped and he reacted too slowly, causing himself to bump up against her from behind and grab her sides for purchase. Again he caught a whiff of her perfume, delicate, unlike himself.

Without any warning his feet came upon a gravelled road and he looked up to find himself close to the house and Hope staring at the many windows. It had three floors and one of the windows on the ground floor was smashed. The guttering was hanging broken and Macleod swore he could see sections of the roof had fallen in.

"Shall we skirt the outside or just go straight in?" asked Hope. "If they are in there, they might run off."

"Run to where," said Macleod. "I don't see any vehicles. And it's miles from anywhere. Come on, let's take a look inside." The pair routed along the gravel track coming to the side of the house which sported an impressive double door. But it had been ravaged by disuse and one side was missing the wooden counterpart that stood on the other side. Macleod stepped through the gap and caught a stench of rotting timber and sodden carpets.

As they made their way down a dark corridor devoid of light,

Hope lit the way with her handheld torch. Although he saw nothing, Macleod swore he could hear rats, scratching away at the walls. Maybe his senses were just on edge. Hope pushed open a door at the end of the hall and light flooded their eyes. Entering and then looking around the room, Macleod saw the remnants of a great fireplace but the hearth was cracked and parts had fallen down. There was a sofa sitting near the fire but it had its insides split open and you could see the springs inside. There was the remains of an old fire on the floor and several beer cans.

"I doubt that's anyone we're looking for," said Hope.

Macleod nodded. "You check out the remainder of this floor, I'll work upstairs. And be careful. I'm not sure how safe this building is."

Hope nodded and he watched her walk away to a door at the opposite end of the room. He found himself watching her until she had left the room but then chided himself that this was not the time or place. Walking back to the hallway, he pulled his own pocket light and found the stairway up to the next level. As he climbed the stairs, he had to tread lightly to avoid the missing steps. As he danced his way up, something caught his eye and he noticed a tin of lip balm on the floor. It was in good condition and he saw no rusting on the tin. A few steps further up, he saw a mobile phone but the screen was smashed.

As he arrived at the middle floor of the house he saw the landing spread out before him and various rooms seemed to lead off from it. However, the floor before him was missing its carpet and the wooden floor beneath was a mess. He dared not set foot on it and he believed neither would anyone else. Macleod continued up the stairs to the top level where again he found a small landing. Half of its carpet was missing and the floor looked as the middle floor but he saw a solid patch on one side and a door to somewhere beyond.

Again stepping lightly, he made his way to the damp wood and pushed it open. There was an eerie creak and Macleod cautiously juked his head inside. The room was small and had a mattress inside, seemingly pulled from a bed in the corner. There were remnants of food which he noted needed collected by the scenes of crime team. But otherwise the room only held broken furniture and old lights. Stepping further into the room, Macleod could see where someone had laid on the mattress and he saw a small plastic container for pills. Picking up the item, he read the side label. Sleeping tablets. *Someone's going on a trip. Why else knock someone out? Why not just kill them here?*

Turning back to the door, Macleod felt his footing give way beneath him and he dropped straight down. His hands shot out and he was caught by his shoulders from dropping any further. The clatter of a floor falling onto the one below set Hope shouting.

"Seoras, are you okay Seoras?"

"No! I'm not." Hearing the floor creak around him, Macleod fought the desire to struggle wildly, fearing it might trigger a further descent. But the floor was most definitely beginning to move. He heard footsteps bolting up the stairs and a few moments later, Hope entered through the door of the room, puffing heavily. She gingerly moved towards him and gave him her hands which he seized gratefully. The whole floor groaned as he was pulled up and out. As he placed a foot on the timber, trying to stand up, it gave way and he desperately flung his arms around Hope's neck, causing her to fall backwards. A large chunk of the timber beside them gave way and he landed on top of Hope who clung to him and tried to roll towards the wall.

Macleod heard the crash as the floor fell away but he didn't feel himself descend but rather, he could hear Hope's heart beat fast as she gripped him tight to her bosom. Having fallen backwards, she had simply grabbed onto whatever part of him she could and they were now in an embarrassing heap. But they were safe, tight up against the wall.

"Thank God no one's here to take a picture," giggled Hope. Macleod knew he should get up but there was the floor to consider that had dropped behind him.

"Sorry, and thank you," said Macleod. "I'd move but I can't actually see where I should move to." Macleod felt Hope adjust herself, probably looking around.

"We'll shuffle backwards toward the door, keeping our weight as flat as we can. Just put your arms out and we'll move together. But stay close to me, don't get up until I say or we might lose the floor."

Macleod nodded and then realised where his head was. If there was a photo of this, it would be circulated around the station like wildfire. There would be many ready to rip on him and his morals and demeanour.

Slowly, Hope began to shuffle backwards and Macleod followed her lead keeping himself close to her but pushing with his feet and hands. He looked up from his position and saw her bruised chin as she worked along the floor with him on top. As they reached the door he clambered over her onto the landing and then stood. Turning around, he helped Hope up, before embracing her.

"Thank you. Sorry for the rather close quarters." He saw

her smile before she started down the stairs and he followed her all of the way out of the house. Once they were standing looking back to the y-boat, Hope dug out her mobile.

"I'll get Allinson onto the roads, stopping any rental vans around here."

"Good, but we should be doing that already," said Macleod. "Do you think we could be seen from the top of the house? I mean be seen approaching the beach down the loch. That room we were in, it's on the correct side to do that. I reckon they would have seen us arriving at the beach. Get a car to come here and pick us up. I am not walking back over there. Besides I don't think we need to be back at the beach. They are running and we need to be on their tail. Tell Allinson we need to find Marie Smith's friends or connections, anyone with boats."

"But does she know we know it's her? She never found the rucksack and pictures. She doesn't know we tracked the rental van. We could just alert her looking at her friends."

"Okay then. Find this van she's got. And get me a car."

Macleod found a rock at the edge of the gravelled track and sat down on it. Before him, Hope was pacing as she spoke to Allinson and he tried to think about other things but her figure grabbed him. Up the stairs, during the fall, it reminded him of something. He remembered walking along an edge, not one with a sheer drop but rather a steep side of a hill. His wife was before him and she had stumbled and he had made a grab for her. They had tumbled together down the hill and when they had come to rest he was on top. They were bruised and battered but when he had gone to get up, she had not let him. And there in the open they had become intimate.

He had been shocked by her abandon that day and he'd

struggled afterwards to let himself go like that again. She had wanted him to but his reluctance, his fear of being caught, of exposure to people's comments. He had hurt her by not letting their play develop, he had stymied her. One more frustration for her from the one person she had never expected it from.

"Car's coming, sir."

"It's okay Hope, you can call me Seoras here. There's no one coming for a bit. Sit down, 'cause you look shattered."

"Well, you will go falling through floors." She let go a little giggle, nervous and forced.

"You've been on the murder team two years now, that correct?"

"Yes, two years."

Macleod nodded. "Is this your first one with a live body to save? You seem nervous."

"Yes, so far they have started off dead and no more have been added. You don't seem to be nervous."

"Inside, I'm churning. Inside I'm falling apart Hope. We need to get lucky and save a woman's life. And I'm stuck here awaiting a car. And all I can do is think of my wife and how this place killed her. Trust me, the professionalism only happens on the outside."

"Has it been long? I mean, since she left you."

"Yes, twenty years. But I still remember it. And you, you bring it all back."

"Me?"

"Yes," said Macleod. "It's just moments. You're like what she would have developed into. But this place held her free spirit down. I held it down. If I stare at times, I'm sorry, but you remind me of what I lost, what I destroyed. I should have been a bigger man and told them to stuff it all. Don't change, Hope, don't change for them, whoever them is. It'll be the death of you."

He saw her puzzled look but she placed a sympathetic hand on his knee. "Car coming, Seoras. Bit off but it looks like one of ours."

"Thank you God for that."

"Yes sir. Thank God."

Chapter 26

In the back of the car, Macleod sat reviewing the case in his own mind, checking in case they had missed anything. Hope was sitting in the front, occasionally talking to the constable driving but Macleod did not hear any of the conversation. He thought about Sara's mother and the sort of woman she had been. Details were sketchy and probably partisan but it looked like she played around a bit. And she came a cropper because of it.

And Sara had seemed the same, actually making money off sleeping with clients from her massage shop. But she had been doing what he did, investigating. In a different set of circumstances would Sara have been different. *Who knows? But to have the determination to find her mother's killer, as she saw it, was something extraordinary. I hope God sees it that way, Sara, but I don't know.*

The radio in the car beeped into life and Macleod listened to the conversation now. A van found and not far from their current location.

"Get me there, now constable."

The driver stepped on the pedal and the car roared along one of the main roads. After a few minutes, Macleod saw a police car, lights flashing at the side of the road. His own car pulled up alongside and he jumped out of the car.

A female officer with a squat face moved towards him. "I checked the van in case anyone was in trouble, sir. But I have only opened the front driver's door and the rear door, nothing else. I haven't touched anything either with my bare hands."

"Good," said Macleod, "much in it?"

The woman indicated he should follow and led him to the rear of the van where one door hung open. Looking inside Macleod saw the blood on the floor. It was not a copious amount, more of a smattering. There were several attempts made to clean up by the wet wipes left in the van. This was looking very amateurish, like a panicked attempt. But where do you go from here? And how? If this was Marie Smith, she'd need an accomplice, someone either to manipulate like she had the poor man who had lost his life at Ness, or an outright player. He doubted the second.

"Officer, get hold of Detective Allinson and tell him to find Iain Angus MacDonald right now. See where he is. Trace his car."

"Sir?" questioned Hope as the officer retired to relay instructions.

"Look at this. Up until now it's all been done rather well. No hint of panic but I reckon she got a shock when we found the beach and then the house. She never expected us to hone in like that. Why would she? We got lucky. Whatever she's done with our young woman, she's been trouble and there's blood in the rental van. I don't even think she knew we were onto anything until she saw us get to the beach. So what does she do?"

"She tries to clean up the van with whatever she's got," said Hope. "There's only wet wipes and there's not enough, so she decides to move on, cut and run. But she needs another vehicle, needs someone she trusts, or at least can manipulate. Her son, he's involved, so blame him."

"That's what I think. But it also means she needs to get rid of our young woman now. She may even come back to torch this. And given her record I think Iain Angus might be in danger too. We need to find her fast. And it'll be dark soon or as dark as it gets here in summer. She might hide up until then. We need to find her fast."

"If she's going to hide until later she will get the car out of sight, surely. Iain Angus' involved in the case if it's him, or she'll use someone else. You should get back to Stornoway and run things from the operations room, sir. It'll be down to the feet on the ground and you'd be of better use there."

Macleod nodded and looked inside the van one more time. There was nothing but smeared blood, wiped down but not all mopped up. There must have been quite a bit to start with. A sickening feeling went through his stomach as he thought of what might have happened in the van. Walking to the front cab of the van, Macleod saw it was completely devoid of anything. He carefully opened the glove compartment with a covered hand and saw it only had the manufacturer's manuals and notes in a smart leather wallet.

She'll come back for this, surely. She'll realise she can't leave it. She'll have to clean it thoroughly at least. But she doesn't know we know about the van. So her priority is to get rid of the body. If the girl's a corpse. If not she'll need to dispose of her. Come on Allinson, give me something.

After catching a car back into Stornoway, Macleod made his way to the investigation room which fell silent as he entered. Hope flanked him as he began what he prayed would be a galvanising pep talk.

"We have a life in our hands, possibly two. I believe our killer is in a panic but still unaware of just how much we know. We've had good presence on the roads and this will have spooked her. She's probably in another vehicle, not her own, and possibly with an accomplice, maybe her son, but I'll keep an open mind regarding that. So we need our road stops, looking for anything unusual, search vehicles if we have to. We need feet out checking outhouses, barns, anywhere you can hide a car. Relatives too. Check her relatives discreetly."

Hope stepped forward and indicated she wanted to talk. Nodding, Macleod stepped back and watched Hope take centre stage. As her hands went to her hips, pushing her blouse back, she cut an imposing figure.

"I know we'd probably like more people than we have but there we go. Most of you are also like the boss and myself, pretty exhausted and more than a little weary from the last few days. However, let's step it up again. Every detail, get it checked, get our foot soldiers on the move and searching. Everywhere Marie Smith might go, find it. This is Stornoway, this is your place. Show us you know it and its people. Find her!"

There was a moment of silence and then people broke. Macleod clapped his hands and there was sudden silence again. "One big push, please. Thank you all for your efforts, one last big push." As the din of the room began again, Hope drew Macleod aside.

"Sorry, was that too much?"

"A little. If we don't get her we can't have this lingering on them. There's a large amount of luck in this and these guys may have to do this again one day. You can't have any hang ups. The Lord knows I have mine and it's a form of hell."

Hope nodded and smiled. "I'll get on it too."

"Relatives, people we don't know that Marie Smith might use. Maybe in an innocent way. Borrow their car. Park somewhere."

"Yes sir."

He hated this time. Macleod had deployed his troops and now he had to wait. Someone gave him a coffee which stopped his first course of action of making himself one. Then a call came in from his boss. After updating her, he came back into the investigation room and tried to look positive. But it was a struggle. After a while Allinson updated him on what they had covered so far. It was all good and useful but had produced no fruit. Outside the evening started to draw in.

He watched Hope swooping around the room, gathering information from different officers. Her bruised face still spoilt her looks but she had a different beauty, a grace about her. And as she was talking to a male detective, he saw her face light up. She grabbed the airwave communications and spoke to someone out in the field. Macleod could not make out her words but her shoulders tensed and her foot began to tap. He reached for his jacket.

Hope raced over to him and then saw his jacket in hand.

"Just take me there and tell me in the car," said Macleod and followed her out of the door.

Hope drove the car from the backyard out into the streets of Stornoway. It was a tight knot around the station with one way traffic flows and she remained quiet as she worked her way out to the main roads.

"Out toward the little wind turbines we saw on the ferry, near the sewage plant," spluttered Hope, "apparently a cousin on holiday, neighbour has seen movement recently."

"Holm direction," said Macleod, quietly and with little enthusiasm. *Right where I was the other day. Where you said goodbye.*

"The neighbour said it could only have been ten minutes since the car left."

"Where did it go? Right or left? Main road or up to the Iolaire monument?"

"She didn't say, I didn't know there were two directions, thought it was a single road in to them."

As the car exited the main part of Stornoway and climbed slightly on the road out, Macleod thought about where they had roadblocks. On the board it had shown one at the school at Sandwick which was just beyond the junction they needed. Anything else was taking the road back to town, in amongst people and familiar faces. Or up to Holm. She's trapped but if she has a body to get rid of, then the sea is the place.

Hope had now climbed out of Stornoway and Macleod pointed to the junction for her turn. She flung the car round and went quickly down the single track road. There were two houses together and a new one just beyond them with a police car outside. Pulling the car up alongside, Hope wound down the window.

"What's the latest officer?"

"Left fifteen minutes ago. I radioed all units in town and at the station. Blue Kia, hatchback. This house is a new build only here a year. Mr and Mrs Smith, currently on holiday in the Bahamas. Car registration starts with an SY but then most cars here do."

"Have you been up to the memorial?" asked Macleod leaning across Hope.

"No sir, I was interviewing the neighbours."

"Go!" Macleod pointed ahead and Hope drove off leaving the astonished officer behind.

"Where?" asked Hope driving on down the single track road.

"Right at the bottom and then follow it to a car park. She might go for the memorial if they have a body, dump it off the rocks down there.

The car pulled round into the car park and they both exited with it parked in the middle. Neatly parked in the corner was a blue Kia hatchback. Hope was quicker and after negotiating the two gate entrance to the path, raced down it towards the Iolaire memorial, a commemoration of an historic shipwreck. As Macleod reached the path, Hope was out of sight and he took off after her. But then he met her coming back up.

"Nothing down there, sir. Just nothing. No signs of anyone there."

The light was fading now and Macleod was struggling to see far. "Back to the top of the path and see if they went across the field." Together they ran uphill, puffing the whole way. Hope reached the top first and looked around.

"Can't see anything. Where should I be looking?"

"Access..., access..., will be over there, somewhere." Bent over Macleod's hand shot out and pointed in a perpendicular direction to the memorial. He tried to stand up but his breath eluded him and he bent back down again.

"There!" shouted Hope. "I see a head, over there."

Macleod looked up. *Over there. No, not over there. That's where she went.* "Go Hope, go!" He hauled himself upright and started to run. Although now night time, the darkness was a twilight and they could see in front of them. What was hard to make out was the surface as it produced stumps of tough grass amongst a boggy base and as she got to the bottom of the hill onto the moorland, Hope tumbled forward, soaking herself in damp peaty water.

Macleod did not look back as he passed her but kept running. He knew she would get up and follow, she was a lot tougher than him but he had run across moors like this as he had grown up and his eyes began to pick out the drier route. If Hope had any sense she would follow him. In the distance were the sounds of sirens, the officer at the house using his initiative, perhaps?

The moorland ran fairly flat with a rolling feel of small humps before it climbed back up across several ditches to the rocks that Macleod knew were beyond. As he climbed to the top of the bank he saw two people, a woman and a man with a canvas sack between about the length of a person. They were swinging it back and forward at the cliff edge.

"No!" cried Macleod. But the pair swung again before letting the canvas bag go. It fell and crashed into the water. Desperately Macleod tried to scrabble down a rocky bank whilst trying to watch the perpetrators of the gross act he had seen. He recognised Marie Smith and watched her walk deliberately and simply shove her son, Iain Angus, into the swirling sea below.

Macleod reached the bottom of the rocky slope and made across the small outcrop, attempting to grab Marie Smith. But she was ready for him and kneed him straight in the groin knocking the wind out of him. She then turned him round, pushing him hard. But Macleod had a grip like a dead man and he held tight to her jacket causing the pair to stumble and fall backwards to the water below.

Chapter 27

The cold of the water caused him to panic and Macleod thrashed about hitting what he presumed to be Marie Smith. He kicked hard trying to surface and found his breath disappearing quickly. With an effort he broke the surface and gasped as he suddenly dropped back down. Something hit him, possibly a foot, but in the water it was hard to tell. He opened his eyes but saw nothing. The salty water was on his lips as he breathed out. Again he sought the surface to grab another precious breath. *A breath she never took.*

Arms at his side pushing down on the water, he managed to get his head above the surface and remain there. Thrashing around, he turned himself towards shore and the small cliff edge behind him. Hope was shouting something. Then she was gone.

He could not see Marie Smith. Then beside him was the bag. Grabbing hold of it, he tried to pull it up and found himself beginning to sink. He had to get this bag to the surface, had to see if she was alive. They had searched for her, now having found her she had to be okay. But his head said different.

"Catch!" Hope was shouting and in the dim light he saw an orange ring land near him. He could not reach it whilst holding the bag. "Get the ring, Seoras, just get the damn ring!"

She was right but how could he let go. She might be alive. "Get the ring or you'll drown, you bloody fool."

He knew she was right. He knew he had to let go. But a part of him just could not. Something made him hold on. His head dipped below the surface again and fought hard to kick up. He still had the bag, still had her, she could still be okay. His head popped back above the surface. He grabbed a breath but a wave came over and he swallowed water. He was choking now. *Kick hard Seoras, kick man.*

His head broke the water and he heard Hope's voice.

"Officer hold this and don't let go."

"You can't. It's not safe. Lifeboat's coming."

And his head disappeared back below the surface. Above the surface, he was sure would have been a loud splash but here underneath, there was the sound of bubbles and something akin to a sudden deluge on the surface. Something had entered the water. There was commotion around him but he saw nothing and began to feel his legs failing, his breath gone and the water he swallowed choking him. He tried to swallow it, to clear his throat but he simply blurted out and swallowed some more.

Someone grabbed his hand and he felt it being pulled above the surface and jammed into a tight area, and a rope cutting across his wrist. Then an arm grabbed him and pulled him upwards, his head breaking the surface. He gasped.

"Bloody hold on, you stupid shit. Just flamin' hold on. They're coming Seoras."

He felt Hope supporting him, her body coming underneath his, holding him up. There was an arm and he was resting on her torso. Then he shivered. It was so damn cold. His mind struggled to think. *What am I doing? Where am I? What is this in my hand? The bag! He had to lift it!*

He pulled with his arm and reached with his other. And everything tipped down into the water. Water filled his nostrils. The bag slipped from his grasp. There were bubbles filling his ears and he could not work out what was happening. Then he was thrust upwards, and someone placed his other hand through a rope. Then his body was driven up and he felt the cold air again. He gasped for breath, choking and spitting.

"Bloody stay there. I'll get her, don't bloody move you clown, or you'll die out here on me."

He lay on the life ring beneath him, feeling the water splash his face on occasion but he could breathe. His body was cold, shivering, but he was breathing better now. Gingerly he tried to glance around but he was more drifting than moving the ring himself. Beyond him he saw a hand. It was slapping the water and trying to pull the rest of its body above the surface. It failed and slipped back down.

Another life ring hit the water beside him and he grabbed it. Moving his feet, he managed to wheel round and saw Hope desperately trying to hold the bag above the water's surface. There were shouts from the water's edge but he struggled to understand what they said. With a push he shoved the second life ring towards Hope and tried to shout. But his voice was lost and he watched the ring bang Hope in the back of the head.

She seemed amazingly calm, though fighting hard, her actions were those of an experienced person. He watched her manage to grab the life ring and then pull the bag half onto it. He saw her face. She was breathing hard, but she looked content. Her life ring was drifting away from him but she showed no panic.

"Hold on," she shouted on seeing him. "They will be coming for us. Don't panic and hold on."

He could only nod. He closed his eyes and clung tight to the ring as he drifted offshore. It was almost tranquil now. Hope had the girl. They could not do anymore until someone got there. Then his mood dropped.

She was here with no one. Alone, she went alone. Dear God, were you with her? Why didn't you put someone useful on the shore for her? She's still here, somewhere down there. How could you? I should have jumped in. Even Hope jumped in. Did you just watch?

The tears welled up in him and he began to shudder. His mind swirled with images of his wife. Her hair drifting in the water behind her as she smiled. And they were embracing, rolling down the hill again. But then they fell into the water. And he was stood with a man in a white, Arab clothing for a hot day, looking down at her sinking.

A hand grabbed his. Macleod was not sure if this was illusion until he felt the cold of the touch send a shiver up him. The face of Marie Smith appeared before him, gasping for breath. She was panicking, barely breaking the surface before descending. He reached. He uncoupled an arm from the life ring and grabbed her. Their hands linked and he felt her weight drag at him.

"Hold on," he shouted. But his words were lost as a helicopter roared overhead. The noise was deafening and the water whipped up as it remained above them. A search light swung about and he looked up only to blind himself. He felt Marie's hand slipping and he tried to grab again. But it continued to slip, so Macleod untied his other hand and was perched over the life ring. He flailed with his second hand and momentarily grabbed her coat. But then she slipped from him, a sudden descent to the depths below.

Macleod was unbalanced and fell off the ring into the sea again. He shot his arms out in a panic, kicked his legs again. His head surfaced into the din of the helicopter and he sought anything to grab. But he started to sink again.

Then a pair of arms grabbed him. He was not sure how but something grabbed his coat at the rear and he was dragged backwards. As he was lifted suddenly upwards, he felt the night chill go across his face and blessed his God for it. Arms grabbed him and he was placed on a hard surface.

"Can you hear me? Can you hear me?" The shout was almost drowned out by the helicopter. Macleod nodded. A sudden thought of Hope made him turn his head and he saw the sea tossing here and there and a woman holding onto a life ring, a canvas bag in her grasp.

Macleod lifted himself up and he was directed inside the lifeboat. The sea made an unsteady platform but an arm supported him into a seat while a face with a ginger beard asked him questions and wrapped him in a silver blanket. Had he swallowed water? Yes, he had. The man kept on talking to him but all he wanted to do was see Hope. He looked outside the rear door he had come through and Macleod saw the canvas bag on the deck. Someone was cutting through it.

As the bag was opened, it appeared to move from inside. A face appeared and Macleod thought he saw blood, dark and crusted. The eyes were closed but he recognised the face of the young woman who he had sat beside. The crew were shouting to each other and he felt the boat speed off.

Sitting back, Macleod was struggling to focus. The man with the ginger beard was still talking to him but Macleod was feeling less inclined to respond. The boat was bouncing along and he was feeling a churning sensation. Suddenly he vomited, catching the shoulder of the man in front of him. The man swore but then wiped the mess off himself, his eyes never leaving Macleod.

A flash of silver moved behind the man and a figure dumped itself into the seat beside. He raised his head. Hope was scanning him, looking to see his face. She was cold, her hair a mess, the pony tail gone and a wild, ragged mass of red flowed out behind her. She let the silver blanket fall from her shoulders and grabbed his head pulling him towards her, cuddling him like a baby.

"We got you. Thank heaven we got you."

Macleod felt the strong wrap of her arms around him and the curtain fell down. Weeping like a child, he shook as he cried, his hands reaching for Hope's shoulders. As she held him, they were buffeted back and forward by the boat bouncing through the waves, one minute lifting and the next thudding through a wave.

The lights of Stornoway town and harbour came upon them but Macleod stayed nestled in Hope's arms. He heard people coming on board and removing the young woman who had been in the bag. They may have been working on her on the way back, he would not have known. But as he felt the boat come to a halt, he forced himself to sit upright and look at Hope.

"What happened to her?" Macleod's finger was pointing at the bag still lying cut open on the deck.

"They were working on her and then took her away. They were still working when she left. Who knows?"

Macleod simply nodded and then stood up. The silver sheet dropped off him and he shook out his trouser leg, making the trousers flap against him.

"Where are you going?" asked Hope.

"Plenty to do. I need to go and supervise this."

"No, you don't. You need to go to hospital and get checked out. Did you swallow any water?" Macleod nodded. "Secondary drowning. You need to go to hospital. Allinson can handle this. We need to get off the boat too. They'll be back out looking for Marie Smith and Iain Angus."

Macleod looked down at the ground. "I had her. She was in my hands and she just slipped out. I lost her Hope. I lost her."

"I didn't see Iain Angus. Did you?"

Macleod shook his head. "She probably killed her own son. What is that all about?"

Hope went to walk past but Macleod stopped her and handed her the silver blanket he had discarded. "You might be a hero but if we are to get filmed, better if we look covered up rather than a scene from Baywatch." They both stepped off the boat and were met by medical personnel as another ambulance left with its blue lights flashing.

Macleod stood on the pier and looked back as the lifeboat turned again out to sea. In the distance the helicopter of the Coastguard could be seen lighting up the night with its searchlight. Around him were men in blue outfits, now clamouring into vehicles and heading towards the helicopter. There seemed to be action everywhere while he seemed to be still.

I nearly joined you. God knows I would have loved to join you.

Chapter 28

Macleod took his coffee and sat down at a table in the leisure centre cafe. The hour was now just after nine and he had agreed to pick up Hope from her early morning swim. Yesterday had been a day of paperwork once he had gotten the all clear from the hospital, and he did not fancy starting this day with more administration.

He scanned the pool for Hope and spotted her swimming up and down on the far side of the pool from his vantage point. She was an extremely competent swimmer, cruising through the water. *Thank you God for that*, he thought, remembering how she had helped save him and how she had managed to keep the bag afloat for so long in the cold sea.

He noticed Hope climbing out of the pool and giving him a wave. Waving back, he watched her walk into the shower and begin to wash down. The woman had been through a lot but she still cut her wonderful figure and he struggled to draw his eyes away. Maybe it was time to allow himself to look. All this time he had been worried about betraying his wife, as if she was looking down on him. She would have been the first to say that Hope was a gorgeous woman.

His mobile rang and he answered a call from his boss. It

was a routine call to see how he was faring. Macleod spoke with a respect but he also made it obvious he was not up for a conversation of length. When he had hung up the call, he looked for Hope again but she had gone to get changed. Sipping his coffee he waited patiently, watching the gym enthusiasts walk past the cafe.

After what seemed an age, Hope appeared dressed in a smart pair of trousers, blouse and boots. He caught her smile as she saw him and he pushed back a chair for her, asking if she wanted coffee but holding up his own empty cup. When she nodded, he made for the till to order before returning.

"Did you enjoy that?" asked Macleod.

"Always good to swim, sir."

"Seoras. Just Seoras. I think I owe you my life."

"You would have done the same. Although you need swimming lessons if you are going to try that sort of thing," laughed Hope.

"Where did you learn to be such a good swimmer?"

"I was a lifeguard before being a policewoman. I'm very at home in the water. But how are you? I mean, really, how are you? To go in where she went in must have been horrible." Hope was smiling kindly, almost pityingly, and Macleod wished she would just smile normally.

"I feel free. Her death was something I haven't faced. My part in it, the part the place played in it, it all just came back in the midst of this. And when I was in the water, I would have been happy to join her. In a better place, I mean. Somewhere where she could be her and I could enjoy that. Our life should have been better, wilder, and freer to do the good things of this life. Not only for each other but also for others."

"That sounds all very quick," said Hope raising an eyebrow.

Macleod laughed. "That's the speech, now I have to live by it. But I think God's given me a chance to change things. But what about you?"

"Yeah, I'm good," murmured Hope.

"You can't save everyone. And she might make it yet. She's got a fighting chance because of what you did. Unlike Smith and her son. I spoke to the Coastguard last night and they say they covered the whole area so they must have gone down to the depths. The searches might continue off and on for the next few days but it's likely they will wash up in the next few months at worst."

"Nothing less than she deserves," snorted Hope. He watched her raise the cup to her lips and then turn to watch the swimming pool.

"We don't always get what we deserve but you are probably right," said Macleod solemnly. "She did kill Carol Hewitt out of jealousy. And when Sara came along snooping to find her mother's killer, I believe Smith initially thought she had found her lover again. But when she had to pay and realised that she was like the others, she started to see the threat. I think Sara wanted to confront her that night when they met out by the loch. Smith planned it to be there."

"Do you think Sara was meeting to tell her she was going to expose her?"

"We'll never know for sure, Hope, but it seems she was either too close or was actually going to reveal Marie Smith to the world. And then of course, Smith realises that Sara has her own lover who knows everything and she sets Macaulay after the young woman telling him he's about to be exposed for using a prostitute. And then she also gets herself a cover story."

"But that ends in a suicide. She caused one hell of a mess.

206

When I interviewed her, I felt like she was going to come on to me to get what she wanted. Manipulative and cold."

"Yes," agreed Macleod, "but also with a strong physical attraction. Anyway drink up, we need to go visit somewhere."

Macleod watched Hope look at him quizzically before she rose from her chair. In his usual fashion, he indicated she should walk in front, something taught to him from his youth. She seemed a little embarrassed every time he did but she acquiesced. His wife had done the same but then she had been raised to accept this too. Surely it was a good thing, a man showing manners to a woman. Macleod never understood why the action brought complaints when women complained men walked all over them. Mystery of the age, he thought.

Insisting on driving, Macleod took the car out of Stornoway before routing down the single track road to the car park they had raced to only two days before. There was still a small police presence but the area had been combed over. Having parked up, Macleod pointed to the far side of the moorland and to the housing for the life ring. He saw an uneasiness in Hope.

"Come on," said Macleod, "we need to do this. Trust me, I'm an old fart at this."

She looked at him and he saw her eyes water slightly before she nodded. As if it had been her idea, she opened the car door emphatically and began to walk towards their target, not waiting for Macleod. With a mix of long strides and out right running, he caught up as she went through the gates to the field.

As the moorland beneath their feet brought up small pools of water causing a splash on occasion when an unwise step was made, it seemed that the place was also starting to seep into Hope. Her shoulders tightened and her gait became less confident. Walking up to the life ring housing, Macleod saw a new ring in place.

"You saved my life by getting this," Macleod said, touching the ring with his hand. It seemed to be a moment to take, and he prayed that she understood he was taking a moment to honour her. "Thank you."

He watched her eyes scan to the sea beyond, to the edge of the small cliff where he had gone over with Marie Smith. Her shoulders started to shake and she began to weep. He stepped towards her and she leant into him accepting his embrace. But she was tall and the action was cumbersome. As she cried, he started himself, realising how close he had been to meeting his maker. When she started to raise her head again, he saw red eyes, slightly lighter in shade than the hair in the pony tail behind them.

"I always take a moment to pray at times like this. Do you mind? I'm just going over to the edge."

Hope nodded but turned away and Macleod walked over to the edge. Head bowed and eyes closed he waited on his maker. *Take care of her. Be with the young girl too, Get her through as it will help Hope. And bring out the dark to the light. Despite the pain, let us see the evil we cause.*

Macleod opened his eyes and looked at the sea which splashed against the cliff edge below. There had always been something soothing about the sea although he doubted Hope would see it that way. Four dead, three since they had got here, all in the water.

"Does it help? Does prayer help?"

Macleod turned round to Hope as she stepped up beside him. Her face was inquisitive, wondering.

"Yes it does. Or rather He does. Although, it's been a rough ride since I was here all those years ago. Although I prayed I wasn't really talking to Him."

"People do that. But you're the first I've heard admit they did it to God." She laughed.

A little forced, Macleod thought.

"It's been good to work with you, sir. They said you were a morbid stickler but you're not that tight. Maybe someone will have a car accident and we can work together again."

Macleod laughed, forcing it himself, but touched Hope's shoulder as she went to turn away.

"It's been my pleasure. You've been a real help, especially with my own difficulties. I doubt I would have gotten that gentle side from the boys in the team. Thank you."

He looked at her and he could tell she was feeling awkward but he didn't care. As he ran his eyes up and down her, his mind was thinking through if it would work. They would say he was just an older man taking on a good looking younger woman. They would make all the jokes. They would probably question his moral stance, question if he was standing by his dogmatic faith. But they worked well together. She was fitter and saw things from different angles. He had the experience to help her develop, the wisdom to round her into one heck of a detective. And yes, if he was honest, he liked the idea of having a good looking woman working beside him. He was a man after all.

"I'm going to ask to have you assigned with me on the next case, Hope. You deserve that, as long as you don't see it as a punishment."

She smirked. "It'll be a pleasure, sir."

"If you don't mind I want to take just a few minutes on my

own to say goodbye to someone I should have said a proper goodbye to a long time ago."

"Of course," said Hope and gave a brief smile before turning away. He heard her walk away, the awkward footsteps across the rocks. But then the sound ceased and he felt he was being watched. Turning around he saw Hope looking at him. Maybe she had been weighing him up as he had done her.

"If you need me, just say," said Hope. "They say these things are hard, so I'm just over the hill if you need me."

"Thank you." Looking at her, he thought her more beautiful than ever before. It was funny how words and actions changed the physical appearance.

"Your wife, you never said her name. Not once did you call her by name. What was it?"

Macleod turned to look out to sea before turning back. "I always felt I had lost her name when it happened, because it seemed wrong to call her by it after what had happened. But now I think I can again because maybe there's a little stirring."

"I don't understand, sir."

"Her name was Hope, McGrath."

THE END

Turn over to discover the new Patrick Smythe series!

Start your Patrick Smythe journey here!

Patrick Smythe is a former Northern Irish policeman who after suffering an amputation after a bomb blast, takes to the sea between the west coast of Scotland and his homeland to ply his trade as a private investigator. Join Paddy as he tries to work to his own ethics while knowing how to bend the rules he once enforced. Working from his beloved motorboat 'Craigantlet', Paddy decides to rescue a drug mule in this short story from the pen of G R Jordan.

Join G R Jordan's monthly newsletter about forthcoming releases and special writings for his tribe of avid readers and then receive your free Patrick Smythe short story.

Goto to https://bit.ly/PatrickSmythe for your Patrick Smythe journey to start!

About the Author

GR Jordan is a self-published author who finally decided at forty that in order to have an enjoyable lifestyle, his creative beast within would have to be unleashed. His books mirror that conflict in life where acts of decency contend with self-promotion, goodness stares in horror at evil and kindness blind-side us when we at our worst. Corrupting our world with his parade of wondrous and horrific characters, he highlights everyday tensions with fresh eyes whilst taking his methodical, intelligent mainstays on a roller-coaster ride of dilemmas, all the while suffering the banter of their provocative sidekicks.

A graduate of Loughborough University where he masqueraded as a chemical engineer but ultimately played American football, Gary had worked at changing the shape of cereal flakes and pulled a pallet truck for a living. Watching vegetables freeze at -40'C was another career highlight and he was also one of the Scottish Highlands "blind" air traffic controllers.

These days he has graduated to answering a telephone to people in trouble before telephoning other people to sort it out.

Having flirted with most places in the UK, he is now based in the Isle of Lewis in Scotland where his free time is spent between raising a young family with his wife, writing, figuring out how to work a loom and caring for a small flock of chickens. Luckily his writing is influenced by his varied work and life experience as the chickens have not been the poetical inspiration he had hoped for!

You can connect with me on:
- https://grjordan.com
- https://twitter.com/carpetless
- https://facebook.com/carpetlessleprechaun

Subscribe to my newsletter:
- https://bit.ly/PatrickSmythe

Also by G R Jordan

G R Jordan writes across multiple genres including dark and action adventure fantasy, feel good fantasy, mystery thriller and horror fantasy. Below are a selection of his work grouped together in their genres, starting with the popular Austerley & Kirkgordon action adventure fantasy. Whilst all books are available across online stores, signed copies are available at his personal shop.

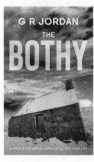

The Bothy: A Highlands and Islands Detective Thriller (Highlands & Islands Detective Book 2)
Two bodies in a burnt out love nest. A cultish lifestyle and children moulded by domination. Can Macleod unravel the Black Isle mystery before the killer dispenses judgement again?

DI Macleod heads for the Black Isle as winter sets in to unravel the mystery of two lovers in a burned out bothy. With his feisty partner DC McGrath, he must unravel the connection between a family living under a cultish cloud and a radio station whose staff are being permanently retired. In the dark of winter, can Macleod shine a light on the shadowy relationships driving a killer to their murderous tasks?

Forgetting your boundaries has never been so deadly!

The Horror Weekend: A Highlands and Islands Detective Thriller (Highlands & Islands Detective Book 3)

A last-minute replacement on a role-playing weekend. One fatal accident after another. Can Macleod overcome the snowstorm from hell to stop a killer before the guest list becomes obsolete?

Detectives Macleod and McGrath join a bizarre cast of characters at a remote country estate on the Isle of Harris where fantasy and horror are the order of the day. But when regular accidents happen, Macleod sees a killer at work and needs to uncover what links the dead. Hampered by a snowstorm that has closed off the outside world, he must rely on Hope McGrath before they become one of the victims.

It's all a game…, but for whom?

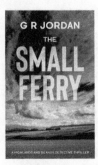

The Small Ferry: A Highlands and Islands Detective Thriller (Highlands & Islands Detective Book 4)
A dreich day for a crossing and a small ferry packed to the gills. After off-loading one man sits dead at the wheel of the last remaining car. Can Macleod find the connections between the passengers, before the killer strikes again?

Macleod and McGrath return to Cromarty when a man is found dead at the wheel of his car on the local ferry. As the passengers are identified, the trail extends across the highlands and islands as past deeds are paid back in full. Can the seasoned pair hunt down a killer before their butchery spreads across the land?

"The Small Ferry" is the fourth Highlands and Islands Detective thriller and brings the odd pair back to the Black Isle when the quiet routine of the Firth is broken apart by a strange death. If you like murder mysteries set amongst the beautiful north of Scotland and its wild coastline and islands, then you'll love the adventures of Macleod and McGrath.

When there's so much going on, it can be hard to see what's happening!

Dead at Third Man: A Highlands and Islands Detective Thriller (Highlands & Islands Detective Book 5)
A landmark cricket club is formed in the heart of the Western Isles. A gala opening leaves a battered body in the changing room when stumps is called. Can Macleod and McGrath find the killer before the rest of the team are bowled out?

In the fifth outing of this tenacious pair, Macleod and McGrath return to the Isle of Lewis when the first match of the newly formed cricket club ends in murder. Uncovering the tensions in the fledgling organisation, they must sort sporting angst from deadly intent if they are to uncover the true reason for the formation of this strange enterprise. Can they discover what bloody crimes sully the perfect whites of the starting XI?

Don't step beyond your crease or you might just be stumped!

Austerley & Kirgordon Adventures Box Set: Books 1-3 and Origin stories 1-3 (Austerley& Kirkgordon)
A retired bodyguard looking for a little fun before it's too late. An obsessive Professor, seeking the darkest things of life. And an Elder god seeking to rule the world, if they can't stop him.

Join Austerley and Kirkgordon on the rollercoaster ride that is their first three adventures. Comprising 3 full novels as well as three accompanying origin novellettes, this collection will introduce you to a polarised duo that are the world's best hope. Joining them for the adventure are a myriad of strange characters, bizarre anmals, evil humans and the UK's finest agents from its most secret department.

As one reviewer put it, "If you like Lovecraft, Poe, or Conan Doyle you will like this book. If you like tv show like Buffy the Vampire Slayer, Supernatural, Being Human, or X-Files you will like this book."

So take a chance on a molotov cocktail of a duo and see how to save the world on the wild side.

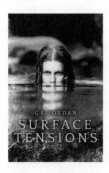

Surface Tensions (Island Adventures Book 1)
Mermaids sighted near a Scottish island. A town exploding in anger and distrust. And Donald's got to get the sexiest fish in town, back in the water.

"Surface Tensions" is the first story in a series of Island adventures from the pen of G R Jordan. If you love comic moments, cosy adventures and light fantasy action, then you'll love these tales with a twist.

Get the book that amazon readers said, "perfectly captures life in the Scottish Hebrides" and that explores "human nature at its best and worst".

Something's stirring the water!

Printed in the USA
CPSIA information can be obtained
at www.ICGtesting.com
CBHW021917250824
13690CB00010B/228

9 781912 153473